BLEACH
Can't Fear Your Own World ___ I

contents

SHUHEI HISAGI

Assistant captain of Ninth Company. Editor-in-chief of the *Seireitei Bulletin*. His interests include guitars and motorcycles from the world of the living.

Nanao Ise

Assistant captain of First Company. She has constantly been at Kyoraku's side as his second-in-command since her days in the Eighth Company.

Shunsui Kyoraku

He succeeded Genryusai Yamamoto as Captain General of the Thirteen Court Guard Companies. He has been friends with Ukitake since they were at Shinoreijutsuin Academy together.

Oh-Etsu Nimaiya

A member of the special royal task force Squad Zero. He supposedly knows the location of every sword in the Soul Society.

Ichibe Hyosube

A member of the special royal task force Squad Zero. He has named many things in the Soul Society.

Nelliel Tu Odelschwanck

An Arrancar. She lost her memories and powers but regained them after meeting Ichigo Kurosaki.

Tier Halibel

An Arrancar and the third Espada. She took over governing Hueco Mundo after Aizen left.

MAIN CHARACTERS

Sosuke Aizen

Former captain of Fifth Company. He betrayed the Soul Society and engaged in a war against the Thirteen Court Guard Companies. Currently imprisoned in Mugen.

Grimmjow Jaegerjaquez

An Arrancar. He developed an obsession when he was an Espada after losing a fight to Ichigo Kurosaki and wants to settle things.

Kugo Ginjo

A Fullbringer and the first deputy Soul Reaper. He led the Xcution group and fought against Ichigo and his team but was defeated and died.

Kaname Tosen

Former captain of Ninth Company. He sided with Aizen to betray the Soul Society because a close friend of his was killed by a Soul Reaper.

Giriko Kutsuzawa

A Fullbringer and member of Xcution. He can manipulate time constraints.

Shukuro Tsukishima

A Fullbringer and member of Xcution. He tormented Ichigo with his powers to alter the past.

Ganju Shiba

Kukaku's younger brother. He rides a boar. He originally hated Soul Reapers but ended up fighting alongside Ichigo and the others.

Kukaku Shiba

Ganju's older sister and a fireworks expert living in the Rukongai. She helped Ichigo and his friends with her unique spiritual powers.

Yukio Hans Vorarlberna

A Fullbringer and member of Xcution. He stole an immense fortune from his father and now runs a large corporation.

Kensei Muguruma

Captain of Ninth Company. He was Hollowfied during Aizen's treachery. He was reinstated to his position after fighting against Aizen as a Vizored.

Shino Madarame

Part of the Thirteen Court Guard Companies. A Soul Reaper appointed to Karakura Town like Ryunosuke. A relative of Ikkaku Madarame.

Ryunosuke Yuki

Part of the Thirteen Court Guard Companies. He was appointed to take over Zennosuke Kurumadani's duties in Karakura Town.

Keigo Asano

Ichigo's classmate and a girl-loving life of the party. Usually hangs out with Mizuiro.

Hanataro Yamada

Fourth Company Third Seat. He helped Ichigo infiltrate the Soul Society to save Rukia. An expert in recovery kido.

Rudobon Chelute

An Arrancar and captain of the Exequias. He vowed enduring loyalty to Aizen.

Mizuiro Kojima

An Arrancar often seen with Loly. They fought alongside each other against the Quincies who invaded Hueco Mundo.

Ichigo's classmate. Popular with older women. He kept his cool carrying out a counterattack while being targeted by Aizen.

Menoly Mallia

An Arrancar often seen with Loly. They fought alongside each other against the Quincies who invaded Hueco Mundo.

Loly Aivirrne

An Arrancar who served at Aizen's side. Tried to hurt Orihime Inoue while she was a captive in Hueco Mundo.

Giselle Gewelle

A Quincy. Also known as Gigi. Giselle's blood turns anyone it touches into a zombie.

Liltotto Lamperd

A Quincy. Her beautiful appearance hides a wicked tongue. She survived Auswählen, but was defeated in the battle against Yhwach.

Bambietta Basterbine

A Quincy and member of the Stern Ritter. Defeated by Komamura and turned into a zombie by Gigi.

Tokinada Tsunayashiro

A member of the Four Great Noble Clans. Part of the Tsunayashiro family.

Hikone

A beautiful child who follows Tokinada.

Ichigo Kurosaki

The main character of the original story.

Can't Fear Your Own World

I

Tite Kubo
Ryohgo Narita

"SEEK NOT
AESTHETICS IN WAR.
SEEK NOT
VIRTUE IN DEATH.
THINK NOT OF
THINE OWN LIFE.
SHOULD THEE SEEK
TO PROTECT THY KING
AND THE FIVE DUKES,
SLAY ALL FOE
AS INDIFFERENTLY AS
SHADOWS OF LEAVES."

—*The Shinoreijutsuin Academy Handbook:
Soul Reaper Regulations Encyclopedia,*
excerpted from an older edition

"DON'T SEEK
AESTHETICS IN BATTLE.
DON'T SEEK
VIRTUE IN DEATH.
DON'T BELIEVE
YOUR LIFE
ONLY BELONGS
TO YOURSELF.
IF YOU REALLY WANT
TO PROTECT SOMETHING,
ATTACK THE ENEMY
FROM BEHIND."

—*The Shinoreijutsuin Academy Handbook:*
Soul Reaper Regulations Encyclopedia,
excerpted from the new edition

PROLOGUE THE FIRST

ONCE, A GREAT WAR RAGED between the gods who claimed to preside over death and those who destroyed the souls of the wicked. After a thousand years of discord, the conflict came to an end when the kings of both sides were brought down. And this great loss became the opportunity to usher in a new dawn for the relationship between Soul Reapers and Quincies. But few knew the real truth that a single person had been responsible for killing both kings— one who was neither Soul Reaper nor Quincy.

The rebels who invaded the Soul Society were known as the Vandenreich, or the Invisible Empire. Their leader was defeated by a boy who served as a deputy Soul Reaper in the Thirteen Court Guard Companies. That scant bit of knowledge, along with the declaration that "the Thirteen Court Guard Companies protected the Soul King," was the only information to be disseminated across the Soul Society.

In other words, news that the Soul King—the very foundation of the Soul Society—had died was withheld to prevent the spread of panic. Residents of the Soul Society, including rank and file Soul Reapers, still believed that the Soul King was enshrined in the Reiokyu, the royal palace. The knowledge of his death was limited to specific Soul Reaper captains, a few higher-ranked seats, and those who held important posts in the Seireitei, all of whom were not especially anxious to destroy the general peace by exposing the truth.

And so restoration of the Seireitei began. Whether the upper echelons of the Soul Society had made the right decision when they chose not to rob the people of their emotional anchor would be determined in the decades and centuries to come.

That last battle later came to be known as "The Great Soul King Protection War." Our story traces back to a time immediately after the end of that conflict.

≡

THE REIO GREATER PALACE, INNER SANCTUARY

There were Royal Guards bustling busily in the spot where the Reio, the Soul King, had once been enshrined. High

Priest Ichibe Hyosube, part of Squad Zero and also the commander of the Royal Guards, silently gazed at the *thing* in the center of the palace and stroked his black beard.

An airy voice called out behind him, "Is that the new Reio, your eminence?"

Hyosube turned to see a man standing there whose right eye was covered by a patch. It was Shunsui Kyoraku. "Ah, looks like you're up and about again, Kyoraku. Mmm, I suppose you wouldn't be the Captain General of the Thirteen Court Guard Companies if you weren't," Hyosube replied with a lively smile.

He realized that Kyoraku's gaze was directed not at him but at the center of the area where the Royal Guards were at work. He replied to Kyoraku's earlier question, "You should already know that the concepts of *old* and *new* don't apply to the Reio. There's value simply in having something here to revere and call Reio."

"So basically you're saying power is all in the name?" Looking conflicted, Kyoraku continued in a politer tone. "In the worst-case scenario, Ichigo would have been sealed to that name."

"Good thing he wasn't, hmm?" Hyosube, his voice free of emotion, offhandedly all but confirmed that there really had been a chance that Ichigo might have been named the Reio. Then, teeth bared in a smile, Hyosube continued to speak of Ichigo Kurosaki. "That young lad caught my interest too. I would have been quite beside myself if he had been rendered silent."

"And good thing too. I wouldn't want Ichigo's friends hating me."

"Ah yes, you gave them soul tickets, didn't you? Let's make sure to keep that a secret from Central 46 and the aristocrats."

"Good grief, nothing slips past you, your eminence."

The Reio's throne was far from a desirable seat, and Kyoraku thought being installed there would have been one of the worst possible endings for Ichigo Kurosaki. He looked at the *thing* in front of him, and the memories etched in his mind flashed once again.

In preparation for that worst-case scenario, Kyoraku had given special spiritual tools called soul tickets to those in the world of the living who knew Ichigo Kurosaki. Soul tickets were talismans that allowed one to move freely between the mortal world and the Soul Society and were the practical result of improvements to earlier techniques that had been used to transfer still-living humans from Karakura Town to the Soul Society.

Kyoraku quietly closed his eyes and remembered warning Ichigo Kurosaki's friends. *"Depending on the type of power it is, it may affect the world of the living. If that's the case, we can't allow him to come back here."*

He recalled the boy who had at first joked around but had then looked intensely angry when Kyoraku explained that it was no joke. *"You're not joking, yet you're telling us to say goodbye just like that?"* Then Kyoraku recalled the boy with black hair whose reaction had been the opposite of the first and who had been immediately angry on Ichigo's behalf. His serene eyes had held an intense belief in Ichigo that had never wavered. Then there had been the girl who had been more concerned for Ichigo's family than herself and who had been deeply distressed on Ichigo's behalf.

Ichigo is blessed when it comes to friends. Well, I suppose he attracts people like Sado and Orihime because he's Ichigo...

Thinking about the children from the world of the living, Kyoraku was relieved that Ichigo Kurosaki was safe now after being the main player in the war's end. Then Kyoraku opened his eyes slightly and spoke to the high priest, an odd statement slipping from his mouth. "More importantly, *I'm glad you and the others didn't kill Ichigo.*"

The high priest neither denied nor confirmed as he laughed heartily and slapped his own bald head. "I'm no Yhwach, after all. I can't see into the future. No, in actuality, Ichigo Kurosaki couldn't have won against him. If anything, we *needed him to lose.*"

"High Priest Hyosube..."

"But luckily for the boy, Yhwach had all of the Reio's power. That guaranteed that the Soul Society would escape destruction whether or not Ichigo Kurosaki won." The high priest faced the *thing* at the center of the Greater Palace and clapped his hands together while he spoke.

At the clear sound of the clap, the high priest closed his eyes and prayed. Kyoraku continued his attempt to question him. "High Priest Hyosube, is that the will of the Reio?"

"Hmm..."

"Or is it just the will of the founders of the five noble clans?"

Kyoraku, whose polite tone had slipped, received an easygoing reply from the high priest. "My my, how can you speak so disparagingly of our dignified founders? Your tone hides none of your animosity. Do you think so little of Byakuya Kuchiki and Yoruichi Shihoin?"

"They've given me no reason to. They're fellow members of the Thirteen Court Guard Companies, and I consider them dear friends." Smiling wryly, Kyoraku shook his head as he continued, tone still casual. "They aren't responsible for the actions of their ancestors, and it's not as if they pretend their ancestors are faultless. Isn't that right, High Priest Hyosube?"

"I suppose you could say that. And none of the founders of the Five Great Noble Clans are still alive, anyway—" Just as the high priest spoke, an explosion echoed through the Greater Palace.

"Huh?!" Kyoraku turned toward the source of the sound, feeling a spiritual pressure markedly different from that of a Soul Reaper. A section of wall that had until moments ago been fused with a Vandenreich building had been destroyed. White smoke was rising from the rubble.

Several humanoid figures whiter by far than the smoke appeared beyond the wall. The Greater Palace Royal Guard immediately unsheathed and readied their swords, but the high priest commanded them to hold. "Oh, no need to worry, everything is fine. You can't win against these ones anyway."

One of the pale silhouettes had already leapt toward them and clucked his tongue as though taken aback. "*Tch*... What? You're not going to fight me?"

Grimmjow Jaegerjaquez, who brought to mind a wild beast, glared at the high priest and Kyoraku with sharp eyes as he landed. "I'm not standing down just because you put away your swords."

Grimmjow's hand went to his zanpaku-to, but a small bala hit him in the back of the head.

"Gah...?!"

The impact was like being punched in the head. When Grimmjow turned to face his attacker, Nelliel Tu Odelschwanck was standing there, left hand still aimed at him. The ram-horned Arrancar woman had arrived in the Soul Society with him and was most likely the one who had hit him with the bala.

"Nelliel, why you...!"

"Is this really the time to pick a fight? Now that the Quincy king's gone, we're the largest group of outsiders in the Soul Society."

"What about it? If you're scared, take that dead weight of yours and go back to Garganta."

The "dead weight" was an Arrancar woman currently leaning on Nelliel's left shoulder. She was Tier Halibel, and both she and Nelliel wore the mark of the Tercera Espada on their bodies.

Halibel had been on the front lines from the moment that the Vandenreich had launched a surprise attack on Hueco Mundo, but Yhwach's overwhelming power had immobilized her, and she had been taken prisoner as a symbol of Hueco Mundo's defeat.

When the Reiokyu had been recreated, Yhwach had thrown her into his own dungeons, and she had eventually come to the palace as a prisoner. Now that Yhwach was gone, no one knew whether he had kept her captive as an example to the other Arrancars or in order to remold her into a vanguard for the Quincies. The only certainty was that she was still alive and had been freed when Nelliel, Ichigo Kurosaki, and the rest of his gang had gone to see her.

Though Nelliel had rescued Halibel, the new king of Hueco Mundo, she had mixed feelings about the current situation. They had been Aizen's followers, and they had first come to the Reiokyu to stand before him here where he had so longed to be. Even as she dealt with her own uncertainty, Nelliel asked Grimmjow, who was hostile toward the Soul Reapers, "You're going to pick a fight with people who've already been worn down by Quincies? That's the kind of fight you like?"

"Tch. You're so naive . You think these Soul Reapers'll actually turn a blind eye to us? I'm not gonna let them stab us in the back on our way out."

The good-natured, bald old man sporting a black beard answered him. "I'll always look the other way when it comes to you. I would even be happy to escort you all the way back to Hueco Mundo."

"Hnngh? Who're you? You're really underestimating us."

The wounded Arrancars were no threat, and Grimmjow assumed that was what the high priest meant. A murderous urge radiated from his whole body as he glared at the bald old man.

"The opposite, the opposite! You're much, much more powerful than any old Hollow. If we carelessly purify or eradicate you the way things currently stand, the balance between the three worlds would collapse."

Grimmjow was briefly silent but soon *tsk*ed as though reaching some internal understanding and held back his animosity. He probably preferred to settle things with

Ichigo Kurosaki as soon as possible rather than waste time fooling around here.

Nelliel guessed his priorities and considered springing a surprise attack on him at the right moment in order to shut him up so she could drag him back to Hueco Mundo. But Halibel, who was borrowing her shoulder, suddenly spoke up. "Is *that* what you're calling the Reio?"

Her words were a whisper, almost as though she were speaking to herself. Her gaze was focused beyond the Soul Reapers at the *thing* enshrined at the center of the palace. "Is *that* the foundation of the Soul Society?"

"Hm. So Miss Arrancar, do you object to it too?" the bald man asked while stroking his beard.

Halibel slowly shook her head. "I'm just a defeated soldier right now. I have no right to comment. But I understand why our late king hated that thing."

Halibel removed herself from Nelliel's shoulder and turned her back on the Soul Reapers. "We've caused trouble for you. We will repay our debt."

"Oh, no worries. The best way for you to repay us is by staying in Hueco Mundo and not causing any more problems. And if you're going to thank anyone, you should thank Ichigo Kurosaki," Kyoraku said as he started to escort the Arrancars out. The women turned to leave the palace.

Grimmjow had interpreted Halibel's comment about debt differently. "Oh, right...! I need to repay that Kurosaki guy."

"You want to finish things with Ichigo while he's wounded?" Nelliel accused. The two continued bickering and squabbling as they left, just as they had been when they arrived.

"Ah well, everyone seems to want a piece of Ichigo— Oh?" Kyoraku noticed that the high priest, who had been standing next to him, was heading out of the Greater Palace.

"Where are you going, your eminence?"

"Just going to give Squad Zero a wake-up call."

Squad Zero. The five members, including the high priest, were said to be as powerful as the entire Thirteen Court Guard Companies put together. They were the elite special royal guard. Each member of Squad Zero was a pioneer who had developed something fundamental to Soul Reaper operations, such as zanpaku-to or shihakusho. They were paragons who had, fittingly, nurtured Soul Reaper history from its starting point of zero.

But Kyoraku had heard that Yhwach and his subordinates had killed all of Squad Zero, minus the high priest, before he made his way to the palace, and so the phrase "wake-up call" left him puzzled. The high priest immediately offered an answer to his confusion.

"We didn't convert our bones to Ôken for the fun of it. Our spiritual powers have more or less fused with the spiritual pulse flowing from our Zero Riden. As long as one of us survives, the others will revive enough to at least walk when they are called for."

"So you would have been in quite a dire situation if Ichigo hadn't won, your eminence?"

Yhwach had at one point remade the Reiokyu into the Wahr Welt—the castle of the true world. Had Yhwach now been alive and well, even the vestiges of the Reiokyu would have vanished and the entire Squad Zero, minus the high priest, would have perished.

"Squad Zero won't die so easily. I won't allow it. That's their fate. And I need Oh-Eetsu and the others to get back to work." The high priest had spoken in an aloof manner just as Kyoraku normally did, but he paused for a moment to stroke his beard several times while looking up at the sky above the palace.

"That whippersnapper has been up to no good while we've been fighting."

≡

THE REIOKYU HOOHDEN (PHOENIX PALACE), HALF AN HOUR LATER

"Oh, this has got me beat." Oh-Etsu Nimaiya had just been brought back from the edge of life and death by the high priest Hyosube. He was holding his head, slumped at the bottom of an ocean even deeper than the subterranean level of the Hoohden—or at least, he was where the ocean would normally have extended across his Zero Riden.

Through the lenses of his glasses, he observed a demolished iron door and the wreckage of sacred ropes and shredded fabric cords. A very specific zanpaku-to was usually sealed away behind that door. But the seal had been ruthlessly destroyed, and there was no sign of said zanpaku-to anywhere.

Taking in the destruction from where she stood next to Oh-Etsu, Mera Hiuchigashima, a zanpaku-to and part of Nimaiya's elite guard, heaved a long sigh. "That's what happens when you let yourself get beat without thinking it through, sir. Seriously."

Normally the sword storehouse rested far from reach deep below the ocean waves, but making Ichigo Kurosaki's zanpaku-to had caused massive evaporation, exposing a significant stretch of the seabed.

"I know it was an emergency, but this sitch went sideways in all the wrong ways," Oh-Etsu said, looking around as he righted his glasses.

Tokie Tonokawa and Nonomi Nomino, also part of Oh-Etsu's guard, were tending to the numerous injured men collapsed all around who had been guarding the sword storehouse.

"That bone-dry ocean was like an open invite to walk right in. Plus me and Sayafushi were out." Oh-Etsu narrowed his eyes, the quiet rage shimmering in them a far different emotion than what had shone forth when he had faced Yhwach. "But what really gets me is that some sleazebag looters showed up during a bona fide Soul Society emergency!"

There was something odd about the wounds the zanpaku-to had suffered. These were among the strongest of the humanized zanpaku-to, and yet areas of their bodies had been frozen, and some were burned or were twitching as though they had been electrocuted, while others seemed to have been poisoned or riddled with holes. A few of their limbs even seemed to have been crushed by blunt weapons.

Mera *tsk*ed at the many unique wounds, each distinctive to a different zanpaku-to. "Seriously, how many people were involved here? If they had that many fighters, they could have at least pitched in during the war."

One of the zanpaku-to who had regained consciousness shook his head at Mera's words. "It wasn't..."

"Hey, are you all right? It wasn't what?"

"It was just one person... The surprise attack... It was all one person..."

Mera was even more bewildered at the other zanpaku-to's words. That wasn't possible, not with all the varied wounds they had.

Oh-Etsu's reaction, however, was entirely different. He narrowed his eyes behind his tinted glasses and spread his hands wide, nodding as though convinced of something. "I see, I see. Well, well, well. Yup, I get it, so that's how it is!"

"You're weirding me out in a whole lotta ways, so could you stop talking to yourself, sir?"

"That's harsh, Mera. Well, that heart-to-heart just helped me pin down the culprit."

Oh-Etsu remained in silent thought as he plucked a shred of binding cloth from the scraps that littered the ground. The cloth looked as if it had been bitten through, and it brought to mind a very specific person. "I wouldn't let a nobody handle one of my swords, but Ikomikidomoe isn't a sword that can be handled by a nobody in the first place."

As he muttered the name of the missing zanpaku-to, Oh-Etsu looked into the empty air with the heartache and outrage of an offended swordsmith but also with a good deal of wariness. "So who are you going to get to wield that sword for you, aristo?"

≡

Then, just as the great battle ended, the Reiokyu's borders were once again sealed. The deadened air resonated with the echoes of combat and the unchanging authority imposed by the Reio, and a great many warnings signaling disaster remained in the atmosphere. Or rather, countless sins continuously suggesting the dawn of a new age in the Soul Society drifted among the pronounced reishi.

PROLOGUE THE SECOND

ONCE, THERE WAS A MAN who lived in the Soul Society and revered a god who had saved his life. This man sought to walk the same path as his god.

Though this man was a commoner from the Rukongai, he earned excellent grades at the Shinoreijutsuin Academy and rose through the ranks until he reached the level of assistant captain. He was steadfast in his honor, loyal to his orders, and never shied from danger if his companions were in peril. He would have risked his very life for the Soul Society.

Yet while he revered fairness, he was callous toward his opponents and more than capable of hiding in the muck to launch a surprise attack, slaughtering and driving back the enemy for the sake of the greater cause.

He was a Soul Reaper.

He gave his enemies death.

He cleansed death from the world.

He transformed the human deaths in the mortal world into salvation.

He was, beyond a doubt, a model Soul Reaper. For better or worse, he embodied the essence of what it meant to belong to the Thirteen Court Guard Companies.

His name was Shuhei Hisagi. He was remembered in the chronicles of the Soul Society as assistant captain of the Ninth Company and had clearly distinguished himself as stronger than ordinary Soul Reapers. But while he was indeed recorded in the chronicles of the Soul Society, there was an unmistakable gulf between him and others who would endure in the stories of the people, such as Shigekuni Genryusai Yamamoto, Kenpachi Zaraki, and Ichigo Kurosaki.

All told, Shuhei Hisagi was considered to be a "very good" assistant captain. He wasn't sure how to interpret that term, which could be taken as praise or ridicule. Either way, he wouldn't change how he lived because his path was already chosen.

Had his decision been made when he was saved by a Soul Reaper? Or maybe in the moment when he had first gripped a zanpaku-to after entering the Shinoreijutsuin Academy? Or was it when he had lost friends during training? Or was it when he had met the man he had decided to follow—the man he had offered himself to, mind and body?

Or perhaps it was when he had killed that man with his own hands.

No one knew when on the journey down his chosen path Hisagi had decided to embrace his life as a Soul Reaper, likely not even Shuhei Hisagi.

≡

SEIREITEI, IN FRONT OF THE FIRST COMPANY BARRACKS

"So, any last words?"

The Captain General's words quietly reverberated around the accused.

The war against the Quincies had been over for a few days, and they had finished eliminating the grotesqueries that had rained down on the Seireitei like strange birds. Although the smell of death had mostly dissipated, the figures in front of the First Company barracks were presently just as tense as if they were in the heat of battle.

Captain General Kyoraku was surrounded by the punishment squad from the deepest level of the subterranean prison, Mugen, and by the captains who had been deployed for the emergency.

Sosuke Aizen, the criminal accused of high treason, had been temporarily released from Mugen for the war. He was now being reimprisoned.

Many Soul Reapers had died in battle with the Quincies, and most of those who had made it out alive were still being treated for their injuries. Although Orihime Inoue had managed to save most of the Soul Reapers who had teetered on the brink of life and death, her Twin-God Reflection Shield was not meant for recovering lost spiritual pressure. She could treat their wounds, but had she tried to fully restore a patient's original spiritual pressure, it would have compromised her ability to save others or to sustain her own stamina.

And so Orihime had been set to treating patients who had been so seriously injured that they had no other hope. Those who had gotten past the worst of their injuries were handed over to the Fourth Company for treatment. Those with fatal injuries who hadn't been reached soon enough, those whose konpaku had completely disappeared, and those who had left no trace of themselves behind couldn't be saved by the Twin-God Reflection Shield. Even Orihime's powers, which had once restored an Arrancar with a blasted upper body, had its limits.

Many lives had been lost and many Soul Reapers had felt powerless nearly to the point of breaking, but news of the ultimate victory had been more than enough to rally the unified and resilient Thirteen Court Guard Companies.

Now they were faced with Sosuke Aizen, and there was no infallible precaution they could deploy against him. They were operating at the highest threat level as they looked out on the prison where he would once again be confined.

Captain General Kyoraku would be venturing into Mugen alone with the prisoner. Although he had asked for last words as a formality, he knew allowing Aizen to speak was dangerous. Even secured to a chair with every part of his body restrained, Aizen could use kido, and his very words could be part of a plot. The Captain General knew that if Aizen said anything threatening, he would need to immediately seal Aizen's voice. Aizen knew that too, and the prisoner shook his head as a brazen smile played over his face.

"Unfortunately, there's no one here worthy of hearing my words. That includes you, Shunsui Kyoraku."

"That's for the best. It's bad luck to be considered worthy by you."

"Though I did want to talk to Ichigo Kurosaki a bit more. Did Kisuke Urahara get the wrong idea about me?"

Ichigo was currently with his father Isshin Kurosaki and Orihime Inoue at Kukaku Shiba's residence in the Rukongai. From a military perspective, it would be best for Ichigo to be there as Aizen was sealed away, but they were taking precautions in case Aizen could influence the Hollow inside Ichigo.

"It turns out Ichigo was never one of us. And if you had something to say to him, you should have taken the opportunity earlier," Kyoraku said smugly, righting his hat and looking down on Aizen with his uninjured left eye.

Though Kisuke Urahara had increased the strength of the seal, they still couldn't be careless. Mayuri Kurotsuchi, just after he had come off of life support, had said, "Can we really count on any of Kisuke Urahara's methods?" Kurotsuchi had attempted to create his own restraint device, but there hadn't been time to wait for it to be completed.

"Let's head out then. We'll just pray you'll be on the Soul Society's side after you've served your time."

"Why say that when you're not sincere?" Aizen smiled as if he could see through everything but didn't even look at Kyoraku as he spoke. "Do you really think the Soul Society will even still be here by the time my sentence has ended?"

"Of course. It's our job to make sure it is."

"You saw it at the Reiokyu, didn't you? You saw the Soul Society's original sin." Aizen was suggesting exactly what his former subordinate Halibel had spoken about, referring to what Kyoraku himself had seen in the Greater Palace of the Reiokyu. But Kyoraku purposefully did not respond and simply headed toward the entrance to Mugen. Even if he chose to answer Aizen's question, he had judged it best to do so in the depths of Mugen, once the voices of the other captains could no longer be heard.

Though Aizen hadn't expected a reply, he spoke sarcastically as though he had seen into Kyoraku's mind, or perhaps into the minds all of the Soul Reapers surrounding him. "Well, aren't you unusually quiet. Are you afraid a conversation with me will cause Soul Reapers to defect? Just like *Kaname Tosen*."

A rage-filled voice echoed through the First Company barracks. "Stop screwing with us!"

It wasn't Kyoraku. This Soul Reaper was a young man with characteristic scars and tattoos on his face, and he was out of breath as if he had just run the whole way there. It was none other than Ninth Company assistant captain Shuhei Hisagi.

The bandages wrapping his entire body hinted at the severity of his wounds, and he looked as though he had until recently been covered with lacerations. He had in fact just slipped out of the Fourth Company's infirmary.

He had been shot by Lille Barro, one of Yhwach's personal guard, and had been on his deathbed with serious damage to his saketsu and hakusui, the organs considered the heart of a Soul Reaper.

But Lille's X-Axis power had been too precise, and Shuhei had miraculously survived the holes that had squarely targeted his body with his primary composition still intact.

Though Orihime had treated Hisagi, she had only healed his wounds, and his damaged hakusui had made it difficult for his spiritual pressure to recover. He had effectively been in a coma for several days, and although he had yet to make a complete recovery, he had come to witness Aizen being reimprisoned. Hisagi had forced himself to run despite being unwise in his condition, in part so that he could see out his duty as the assistant captain of the Ninth Company.

Hisagi's superior, Ninth Company captain Kensei Muguruma, had been zombified and was in a state of suspended animation. He had been placed in one of the Twelfth Company's special treatment capsules to revive. That was specifically why Hisagi, who could barely move, was trying to make sure that at the very least he would be part of the guard at the event.

Hisagi's other reason—one that he was not wholly aware of—was that he wanted to personally see the enemy of his former captain, Kaname Tosen, imprisoned. His heart should have recognized that once Aizen was reimprisoned, all the loose ends would be tied up. He shouldn't complicate matters with his grudges.

Hisagi's hands had been gripped into firm fists as he tried to control himself, but his resolve had collapsed the moment he had heard Aizen's words as he ran up. "Are you saying that you twisted Captain Tosen's views with your words...?"

"What a strange way of putting things, Shuhei Hisagi." Aizen's mood was imperturbable in the face of Hisagi's unconcealed rage. "You never saw Kaname Tosen's mind change even for a moment, did you? That's because Kaname Tosen was serving me by the time you became a Soul Reaper."

"...!"

Kyoraku interrupted to chide Hisagi. "Shuhei, you're right to be angry, but I'm sorry. Can you keep yourself in check right now?"

"Yes, I understand, Captain General."

His hand had been about to reach for his zanpaku-to, but Hisagi quelled the impulse. He said to Aizen, "You might have battled alongside Kurosaki to defeat Yhwach, but you'll be Captain Tosen's enemy in my eyes forever, no matter what happens."

Revenge.

How many times had that word come to mind when he heard Aizen's name? It was something he viewed as simultaneously negative and positive. His heart harbored hatred for Aizen, who had without remorse led Tosen down the twisted path that had brought about the former captain's ruin. But Hisagi also felt swirling doubt and frustration at himself for being a prisoner to his own intense, destructive emotions.

For Hisagi, who had done all he could to stop a revenge-obsessed Tosen from going down the wrong path, letting that word slip past his lips was nothing more than an affront to the Soul Reapers like Komamura, who had fought alongside him, and even more so to Tosen.

Aizen smiled faintly as he strung together his cruel words, as though he could peer straight into Hisagi's heart. "*Forever* is a word that shouldn't be uttered so lightly. Even Tosen's conviction wasn't eternal, after all."

"Gah! How dare you—"

Aizen overrode Hisagi's indignant shout. "You seem to have the wrong idea." His voice was quiet, but it held such definite *power* in it that Hisagi's shout was overwhelmed.

"I did not kill Tosen as punishment for defeat." He paused for a moment.

Aizen ignored the confusion around him and spat his thoughts out curtly, "It was my version of mercy."

The air around them seemed to freeze.

Hisagi wasn't the only one who couldn't immediately grasp Aizen's meaning. Kyoraku and the Soul Reapers around him were likewise at a loss.

A short silence followed, then Hisagi spoke, clenched fists shaking. "You call *that* mercy?"

Aizen seemed pleased at that, and Hisagi's anger boiled all the more. But this anger wasn't directed at Aizen. It was directed at his own weakness compared to the man who had so easily killed Kaname Tosen.

"How much of a fool do you need to make of Captain Kaname before you're satisfied...?"

Aizen was persistently indifferent as he continued. "It was clear that Orihime Inoue or Retsu Unohana would have tried to save Kaname Tosen once they arrived. I don't think any of you could understand what that would have meant for him."

"...?"

"If Kaname Tosen had lived, he would have plunged into an unparalleled despair, and his mind would have fallen to ruin. I couldn't bear to allow someone with such beautiful resolve to waste away in despair. That's why I bestowed on my most loyal subordinate such a merciful death. It was nothing more than that."

Hisagi couldn't understand what Aizen was saying. But he didn't think Aizen was making up some random explanation to trick them.

Ignoring Hisagi's bewilderment, Aizen addressed his next words to the Soul Reapers around him. "Eventually the time will come when you will all understand. The Soul Society, the Soul Reapers themselves, are based on nothing more than a treacherous fantasy."

"How about we end things there? You talk too much." Kyoraku stopped Aizen from continuing and gave directions to the punishment force to start transporting Aizen into Mugen's maw.

"Please wait, Captain General! What the heck is Aizen—" Second Company captain Soi Fon stepped in front of Hisagi as he spoke. She quickly circled around his back and twisted up his arm.

"Get ahold of yourself! You're not the only person who lost a friend because of him!"

"*Guh*! But, Captain Soi Fon—!"

"If someone like you could get revenge on him, we would have executed him by now! He's just trying to get you to act out and cause chaos for his own amusement!"

Hisagi was more painfully aware of that truth than anyone. He was nothing compared to the powerful being that was Aizen. What could someone like him, who had been so upset by Aizen's mere *words*, do?

Though he hated the man, Hisagi couldn't kill Aizen. But he could not forgive or forget what had happened either. Hisagi already understood that well enough.

Aizen, whose body had been restrained in the chair, tilted his head slightly as he turned his gaze toward Hisagi. "'Swinging a sword for duty alone is what a captain does. To swing a sword out of hatred is just violence.' Toshiro Hitsugaya once spoke those words to me."

"Urk..." Hisagi could only be silent. It felt like Aizen was telling him that he was far from captain material, which was something he himself thought. But he could only turn his eyes down and grind his teeth instead of arguing.

Aizen didn't even allow Hisagi the luxury of frustration. "Don't worry about it. What you feel isn't hate. It's just sentimentality for Kaname Tosen and what he left behind."

"What did you say?"

"You would do well to remember this: Regardless of how firm your resolve is, you can't defeat the strong with sentimentality alone."

"Huh?!"

Kyoraku clapped his hands together firmly as though to cut off the conversation. "All right, all right, I said that's enough already, didn't I? Could you stop intimidating the kids hauling you around with your spiritual pressure? You said it wasn't worthwhile to leave any last words, didn't you?"

At Kyoraku's words, the other Soul Reapers looked at the members of the punishment force who were carrying the restrained Aizen in his chair. They couldn't seem to move and were dripping with sweat.

"It's all just a show. I'm going to be quite bored for a while, so I'm entertaining myself with the presumption that my modest words might have the slightest effect on the future of the Soul Society."

"Good grief, that's not what I call a decent pastime."

Finally, the members of the punishment force were liberated from Aizen's spiritual pressure and desperately steadied their breaths as they started forward again.

In the moments before they disappeared underground, Aizen flung words at the assembled Soul Reapers as though he were testing them, his voice as quiet as it had been in the beginning. "If you want to see through to the truth, you must flounder and sacrifice your own flesh, blood, and soul."

Then lastly, and possibly redundantly, he added one final statement for Shuhei Hisagi's benefit, who stood by dumbstruck. "At least that's what Kaname Tosen did. Maybe you should know that?"

And so the monstrous criminal, who had defeated Yhwach alongside Ichigo Kurosaki, disappeared into the shadowed depths.

Aizen took a farsighted view of the world and hadn't spoken like an abject prisoner. It made many of the Soul Reapers scowl because they thought his words were born of the arrogance of a sore loser. The captains, however, centered themselves and held in the corner of their minds the thought that "although he lies for sport, Aizen isn't one to say things without a purpose."

Hisagi had not been able to restrain his emotions at the end, and Aizen's words became a poison that lingered in his heart. The poison didn't warp him, it altered fate itself and eventually led him toward a singular conflict. But that fate might have been inevitable for a Soul Reaper following in Tosen's footsteps, regardless of whether Aizen's poison had found a mark.

Shuhei Hisagi was neither a prophet nor omniscient and so naturally had no way of knowing his future. He wasn't a hero who would go down in history like Ichigo Kurosaki.

He did not have the brute strength of Kenpachi Zaraki.

He did not have the wisdom of Kisuke Urahara.

He did not have the skills of Mayuri Kurotsuchi.

He did not have the status of Byakuya Kuchiki.

He did not have the talent of Toshiro Hitsugaya.

He did not have the experience of Genryusai Yamamoto.

Nor the brilliance of Shunsui Kyoraku.

Nor the drive of Sajin Komamura.

Nor the courage of Kensei Muguruma.

He was the type who derided himself over drinks by saying, "Whether I try to become a captain or stick to being an assistant captain, I can't even list all that I'm lacking," He had few heroic qualities, especially when it came to his own self-respect as a Soul Reaper.

Shuhei Hisagi still did not have the slightest clue.

He had not even the slightest inkling that he would be the one to shoulder the fate of the world as he fought to protect the common qualities that served as the foundation for most of the Thirteen Court Guard Companies.

He came to face that reality just barely half a year after the great war ended.

CHAPTER ONE

SEVERAL CENTURIES AGO,
SEIREITEI GOVERNMENT DISTRICT

"WHY? WHY WON'T YOU EXECUTE HIM?" It was a cry of
desperation.

"Please let me have an audience with the Central 46!
I beg you!" The lone young man continued to raise his
voice despite the obstruction of the sturdy guards bearing steel staves.

The young man's eyes were colorless, and one could infer
from their subtle movements that they saw nothing. He
seemed to grasp the situation around himself solely from
sounds and sensations and likely sensed the brusque attitude of the guards in front of him. The guards, who were
possibly related to the nobility, had clear contempt in their
eyes for the young man, who appeared to have come from

the Rukongai. But the young man was not timid as he tried to stretch toward the inner reaches of the gate.

Cries for a judgment of guilt came flying out of the blind young man's mouth—a genuine entreaty for a just execution. The gate guards would not lend him an ear, however, and swung their staves at him.

The young man heard the sound of fabric being grazed, of air swishing and the flow of footsteps. He perceived all of it and surmised that the guards were going to pummel him without mercy.

But he did not try to evade them. Was it despair or sadness that appeared on his face? He showed not even the faintest flinch of fear. He had been prepared to risk his own life from the moment he had arrived.

The guards didn't notice his resolve, and believing that his blindness prevented him from evading them, they brought their weapons down on their defenseless opponent without hesitation.

The sound of a harsh collision rang out, and the guards' strikes were sent flying back!

A still-sheathed zanpaku-to appeared before them. The guards' expressions froze the moment they recognized who wielded the weapon.

"There's no need to be so rowdy. He's still mourning Kakyo."

"Y-you're…"

"I will talk to him. You should return to your posts."

"Y-yes sir!"

The young man couldn't figure out what had happened. His thoughts were overrun by the name his savior had uttered.

Kakyo.

The reason he had risked his life in coming there. The name of his irreplaceable friend with whom he had spent his youth in the Rukongai.

The man who had said her name spoke gently to the blind man. "I know who you are. You came to Kakyo's funeral, didn't you?"

"Did you know her...?"

"We were colleagues of a sort. I'm a Soul Reaper too. But I suppose I failed in my duty the moment I wasn't able to protect her."

The man spoke with a sorrowful air and offered a hand to the blind man. "Let's go elsewhere. You have nothing more to say to those pigheaded guards, do you?"

"I see, so you're Kaname Tosen. She occasionally talked about you in the barracks. That's probably why you received a special invitation to the company funeral."

The blind man—Kaname Tosen—was a resident of the Rukongai. Since he was not a Soul Reaper, he normally would not have been able to come and go freely in the Seireitei. He had been allowed to enter by special arrangement.

"Kakyo wrote out a will when she enlisted as a Soul Reaper. The Shinoreijutsuin Academy actually recommends it. She had no way of knowing when she might die during a battle with a Hollow, after all."

According to the Soul Reaper who claimed to know Kakyo, her will had stipulated that she be buried in the Rukongai. "Apparently she said she wanted to be buried at the foot of a hill where she could see the stars, and that her close friend Kaname Tosen would know where she went."

"Yes, I think I know that hill."

Memories of looking up at the night sky with his friend, near a village that had once been on top of a hill, flooded Tosen's mind.

"I love the night sky, Kaname. It reminds me of the world. Everything's covered in darkness. There are tiny points of light everywhere, but the clouds try to cover them up.

"You see, Kaname, I want to clear away those clouds so that not a single light is hidden. I'm going to clear away those clouds, Kaname."

The woman who had looked up at the stars and said those words had eventually fulfilled her dream. She had obtained the power and position to protect the world's light as a Soul Reaper.

Soul Reapers were the foundation of everything in the Soul Society—they led the inhabitants of the world of the living here and maintained the cycle of souls.

They drove away the evil souls called Hollows. They were the people's hope.

She had been given the right to literally protect the stars. But although her dream had come true, she had not been able to take her next steps.

"I heard that it was her husband who killed her."

"Yes, that's right. Her husband killed a colleague in his company over a trivial dispute and then killed her when she tried to protest. That is the truth."

"Why did she... Why did someone like her have to die?"

"This is only a guess, but she was more honest than anyone, and I think it's because she kept justice and peace close to her heart," the Soul Reaper replied to Tosen, whose fists were clenched in frustration.

Tosen also understood that.

Kakyo, his best friend, had loved peace more than anyone. She had prized justice more than anyone. That was why she had been prepared to stain her hands with the blood of Hollows she slew herself.

"I was concerned that this would happen to her someday. She loved peace too much to carry out justice. If she had rejected love and peace and lived only for harsh justice, she probably would have killed her husband instead. But she wasn't capable of that."

"Are you saying that her dreams were wrong?! I heard her killer isn't even being charged with a serious crime!"

"Is that why you sought an audience with the Central 46?" The Soul Reaper breathed out a small sigh and continued as if hesitant. "Do you know about the Five Great Noble Clans?"

"I don't know their names, but aren't they the highest-ranking families in the Seireitei, even among the aristocrats?"

"The man who killed Kakyo is a member of the Five Great Noble Clans."

Though he had known she had married a Soul Reaper, he hadn't heard she had married into a family as distinguished as one of the five noble clans.

The Soul Reaper kept talking to the bewildered Tosen. "He isn't part of the main family, just a descendant from one of the branches. So he doesn't have any significant authority. But a man can get a reduced sentence for murder if he is an aristocrat. Had he been part of the main family, they might have just pretended no one had died or claimed that Kakyo had been executed for treason."

"But! But... That's preposterous...!" Tosen unintentionally raised his voice.

In his heart he had considered the possibility the moment he had heard that the man who had killed his friend would receive nothing more than a slap on the wrist. But he hadn't wanted to believe that the organization his friend had proclaimed "power for the sake of justice" could let something like that happen. That was why—because he didn't want it to be true—he had risked his life and ventured all the way here for a personal audience with the Central 46.

"Isn't a Soul Reaper—aren't the Thirteen Court Guard Companies meant to protect the peace of the Soul Society and the world of the living?! Aren't the Central 46 meant to embody the world's logic?!"

"They did protect the peace. The nobles are a part of the world, and they protected *their* peace. The current Central 46 symbolizes that absurd world."

"What?!" Tosen froze in bewilderment at the Soul Reaper's declaration.

The Soul Reaper's face contorted with regret as he said, "I am painfully aware of how you feel. No matter how you look at it, charging the man who killed her with a minor crime makes no sense. But that's the Soul Society. The Central 46 are the five noble clan's yes-men, especially when it comes to the powerful Tsunayashiro house."

The man spoke sorrowfully and clenched his fists just as Tosen did. After he made sure no one was near them, he asked in a quiet voice, "Based on all of that, there's something I'd like to ask you specifically, since you were her closest friend."

Though Tosen's heart had been incessantly gnawed at by anger, he closed his mouth and listened to the man's words as though overawed by the man's earnest tone of voice.

"If either of us had the ability to seek revenge, should we actually go through with it?"

"That's—"

"It's an issue of how we treat her wishes and what we do to honor her. Do you think that she ever wanted you to seek revenge, Tosen?"

Though Tosen could not see the other man's expression, he could sense violence creeping into the Soul Reaper's words. Oddly, it allowed him to regain his composure.

He was barely able to suppress his own anger as he strung together a sentence while recalling his friend's words. This world was far from what she had wanted if her colleague spoke with that kind of hostility in his voice. He desperately tried to reach an understanding within himself as he replied to the Soul Reaper's question. "I don't think she would want revenge. And if that's how she felt, then I..."

But he stopped there. *Then I don't want revenge either.*

He couldn't manage to say it, even to himself. He knew she would never have wanted another person to sully their hands seeking revenge for her. But the emotions pulsing deep in his gut wouldn't accept that as justice.

Her wishes have nothing to do with this. Seek revenge for yourself.

The lump of darkness that bubbled up within him was appealing, but Tosen could not follow that voice. Because he knew. The moment he or anyone else chose to follow that hatred, she would die again.

It would be like trampling on all the proof that she had ever lived. He would be snuffing the life out of her wishes with his very own hands. He could not do that. By purging his own emotions, Tosen was able to string together his next words. "I...would like to respect her wishes for peace and justice."

"I see. You're right. She certainly did love peace. That is exactly why she lost her life, but... But I don't believe she was weak because of that."

The hostility had ebbed from the Soul Reaper's voice, and he spoke now with detachment. "If we can prove that her dream was a strength rather than a weakness, how will you live your life from now on?"

"..."

"Please take up the torch and uphold her dream. Make sure no more blood is shed in vain."

Tosen could not accept the Soul Reaper's words at his core, but he realized that this man had understood his friend the same way he had and was thankful to the man for preventing his heart from being permeated by hatred. "Thank you very much."

"No, I need to thank you since you are upholding her wishes."

"I don't think I have it in me to do that." He wasn't capable of protecting her dreams when even now he was desperately suppressing the rage and hatred that bubbled within him.

Even as the thought settled in Tosen's mind, the Soul Reaper spoke to him with a kind smile. "You don't need to have it in you to uphold her dream. She once said, 'My hope isn't anything special. It's just a paltry wish to protect something that continues to shine like the stars in the sky.'"

"..."

If she had spoken of that, she must have truly given her hopes to her Soul Reaper colleagues to embrace, this man included. Having determined that, Tosen was relieved that there were Soul Reapers who respected her virtues.

"Um...if you would be so kind, what is your name?" He asked so that he could etch into his heart the thought that the world wasn't cruel. There were others who had seen her for what she really was, and the world was not merciless.

The man gave his name in a calm voice without hesitation. "Yeah, my name is Tokinada. Tokinada Tsunayashiro."

"Yes, so...Mr. Tsunayashiro...?" Tosen's mind froze for a moment. He had a strong sense of something amiss. He remembered hearing that name earlier from this very man.

No, it can't be. I must have misunderstood.

When the man saw Tosen's expression as he tried to ask his question again, the man shook his head. "You haven't misunderstood or misheard, Kaname Tosen."

"Huh...?"

"Of course you wouldn't find my face or my voice familiar. Well, I suppose it's fortunate you didn't ask for my name from the start. I don't like using false names."

"Um, what are you trying to do...?" Though Tosen was bewildered, his gut instinct kept shouting conflicting commands at him.

Kill. Run.

Hatred and fear jumbled together in his body and began to circulate through his blood. But his ability to reason was unable to catch up with instinct, and Tosen could not go through with either action.

The man dispassionately reminded Tosen of his position. "I'll tell you again. I am Tokinada Tsunayashiro. Although at this point, I suppose I should call myself your closest friend's nemesis."

"..."

"I'm so relieved you don't want revenge. It's much more terrifying to be hated by a Rukongai urchin with nothing to lose than by another aristocrat who thinks twice about how to protect themselves," the man said. He placed his hand on Tosen's cheek. His smile remained unwavering, and Tosen was assaulted by a chill he had never felt the likes of before.

His whole body was penetrated by heavy, persistent, ominous spiritual pressure of a completely different nature than what he had felt from his friend. It paired with his internal impulses through brute force. It outstripped his fear and even eradicated the instincts yelling at him to *run*.

"I was planning to kill you if you had answered that you wanted revenge for Kakyo. Talking with a fool who didn't understand her would have been quite unpleasant. It would be one thing if you were another Soul Reaper, but I won't get in trouble no matter how many Rukongai inhabitants I kill."

Tosen realized that the hostility he had felt in the man's earlier words had been aimed at him, but that didn't matter anymore. He couldn't even understand what the man was saying. He didn't want to understand. But the man had made Tosen's emotions explode, and that was more than enough to liberate him from the fear that weighed down his body.

The man who declared himself to be Kakyo's nemesis was right there in front of him. Tosen didn't care whether it was true or not. He couldn't forgive a man who was willing to harbor such a sinister intention against another human being for even mentioning her name.

The negative emotions he had suppressed in his depths burst forth and he attacked the Soul Reaper Tokinada Tsunayashiro.

"Hhhhhhhhhhhhhhhhhgh!" His scream was no longer human. With a cry like a beast, Tosen grabbed at the man in front of him. However—

"Good friend of my wife, why do you rage so?"

Tosen's world flipped forcefully upside down. His back hit the ground and he couldn't move. The taste of blood spread through his mouth, and he realized his limbs were paralyzed from intense pain. Even so, Tosen tried to get up.

From above him a calm voice continued to resound. "My wife Kakyo would have forgiven me."

"You...you... You...!" Though Tosen tried to yell in the direction of the voice, his throat, now filled with blood, would not allow him to form words.

"Don't you remember how you answered earlier? You said you'd respect her wishes. If you care for my wife, shouldn't you forgive me, forget your hatred, and live your days in the peace that we Soul Reapers protect?"

"Guh!"

"I think that's what my wife would wish you to do. Try to understand for her sake."

Tokinada pressed his sheathed zanpaku-to to Tosen's neck as the young man tried to get up. He pushed Tosen to the ground, crushing his throat. "Although it's not like someone who can't even use a single form of Soul Reaper combat even has the means to seek revenge."

Then he called to the guards who had gathered at Tosen's shouts. "Hey, all of you. I've got a job for you. A resident of the Rukongai tried to raise his hand to me. Get him out of here—quickly."

"Y-yes sir!" The guards felt something like dread when faced with a smiling member of the five noble clans ordering them about, although they still followed his directions.

As though trading places with the guards, Tokinada left Tosen's side. Then, as though he had just thought of something, he said, "Oh, let me spell this out for you so you don't have any misconceptions. Nothing I said was a lie. It really is a strange world where a man like me doesn't get punished. I do think it's unfortunate that Kakyo couldn't be protected from the unreasonableness of the world, and I understand that her dreams were noble."

"—"

Tosen tried to yell something through his crushed throat as he glared at Tokinada. Even blind, he could clearly see the atrocious smile filled with joy and malice fixed on the face of the departing Soul Reaper.

"It's just that I found her dreams so loathsome they sickened me."

More than anger at the man, Tosen felt a deep despair at the world that had trampled on his friend's dreams. The stars that she had gazed up at hadn't illuminated her at all. She had been the one bringing light to the world, and now she was forever lost. The guards' staves rose once more over Tosen, who was engulfed in intense misery and rage.

This time, there was no one to stop them.

≡

PRESENT DAY,
SOMEWHERE IN THE SEIREITEI

"Hm..."

Somewhere in the Seireitei, a man awoke.

"Ah, I just had the most nostalgic dream." He stretched in a luxurious, throne-like armchair and turned his eyes toward his gloomy surroundings.

The petite figure of a child immediately came into view. Eyes glittering brightly, they raised their voice to ask, "Are you awake, Lord Tokinada?!"

"Yes, I had a lovely dream. A sign of good things to come."

"A dream? What kind of dream, Lord Tokinada?!"

Prompted by that childlike voice, Tokinada Tsunayashiro considered his recent dream, "Hm." A wicked smile twisted his mouth as he answered. "It was a nostalgic, pleasant dream. It's vivid even now. The instant someone else's heart is filled with despair is the instant my chest clears. I never grow bored of the moment I strangle the boundless hatred for me out of someone, no matter how many times I experience it. Even when it's just a dream."

"Do you? I don't really get it, Lord Tokinada!"

"That's fine. You don't need to understand. You're still young."

The child wore black garments that bore a striking resemblance to the shihakusho uniform of a Soul Reaper but no armband designating a company. They also behaved unlike any other member of the Soul Society.

They were probably around fifteen, if measured in the way of the world of the living. And while no one would argue that the child was a beauty, their androgynous face made it impossible to determine their gender.

"What were you doing, Hikone? Surely you weren't just standing there until I woke up."

Hikone smiled innocently as they responded. "Yes! I did just exactly as you told me, Lord Tokinada! There were people who came to kill you, so I made sure they couldn't move!"

Tokinada once more surveyed the scene around him. There were several people in black clothing collapsed around Hikone, many of them twitching with pain because all the bones in their limbs had been broken.

Based on their attire, Tokinada deduced that they were assassins hired by the nobility for their covert abilities. Tokinada slowly stood from his chair and gave Hikone a light pat on the head. "I see, very good. You did well."

"I did! I did! Thank you so much, Lord Tokinada!"

Paying Hikone no mind, whose eyes glistened like a puppy's, Tokinada slowly approached the assassins and stood in front of one who appeared to be still conscious. He asked casually, "Can't you tell your clients are all dead? Why are you still trying to be faithful to your assignment?"

Tokinada glanced behind himself as he spoke, where several aristocratic figures were seated in chairs around a long table. Their robes all bore the same family crest. It was the same crest Tokinada himself wore, and so they must be part of the Tsunayashiro family. Yet none of them moved. Every person at the table had either their throat or their stomach slit open, and all it took was a glance to determine that they were dead.

"Assassinate Tokinada Tsunayashiro. Normally you'd expect an order like that to come from the other leaders in the Tsunayashiro family. But as you can see, they're dead. Why couldn't you have taken this opportunity to simply abscond with your advance?"

The assassin remained silent. He might have been trying to avoid revealing even the slightest bit of information about himself or his colleagues, but Tokinada realized when the assassin didn't attempt to commit suicide that he was still looking for an opportunity to hit his mark.

Having made that determination, Tokinada happily let his mouth relax and slowly brought his hands together as he clapped in admiration. "Amazing! My respects to your tenacity in carrying out a mission regardless of whether your client is dead. I would absolutely never do that."

As the assassin continued to glare at him, Tokinada said, "Yes, and as your reward, I'll let you in on something.

Your client is still alive. In other words, your actions were not in vain."

The assassin scowled from his heap on the floor. Though it had come through an intermediary, the assassin had assumed that the order to assassinate Tokinada had come from a member of the family who shunned him.

But he had the strange sense that something was off after Tokinada completely contradicted his earlier statement that "Can't you tell your clients are all dead?" He waited for Tokinada's next words and an opportunity to kill him.

A smile, as if he were humoring a child, settled on Tokinada's face. "It was me."

"...?"

"I gave the order for my assassination."

"...?!"

Tokinada continued to explain to the bewildered assassin. "I turned the tables on the assassins sent to murder the Tsunayashiro family, only to discover that they were all already dead! I've found a wonderful way to gain sympathy, haven't I?"

"Impossible!" The assassin's face contorted at Tokinada's claim that he had made them all dance on the palm of his hand.

The intermediary had always been the same man—a protégé of the Tsunayashiro family. He wasn't aligned with

Tokinada, whom the family viewed with the same affection they would show a tumor.

Tokinada's next words seemed aimed at mocking that assumption. "You seem confused. Well, I don't care if you believe me or not. Assassins like you are often full of despair already. It's a lot more fun to confuse you."

"What...are you...?"

Tokinada laughed as the assassin tried to squeeze out his words. "Why am I going on about all this? Doesn't it strike you as foolish for me to tell anyone my plans, even if no one can bring the Twelfth Company's rokureichu recording spirit bugs into the residence? Do I look like a fool?"

Then Tokinada put his foot down on the assassin's fingers and crushed them.

"Gaah...!"

Tokinada smiled, laughed, and cackled happily at the sound of the bones breaking. "But I just can't help myself! I suppose it's a bad habit. Even at the risk of being overheard, I just needed to see it! I needed to see the bewilderment on the face of a prideful assassin like you! That expression on your face!"

Methodically and leisurely, Tokinada smiled as he stamped on and broke every bone in the assassin's body over and over again.

Suddenly the grin wiped from his face, and he calmly shook his head and spoke to himself. "Though if you think about it, you would never have become an assassin for the aristocracy if you'd had any pride."

He breathed a small sigh and pulled his zanpaku-to from his hip.

The glitter in Hikone's eyes didn't waver as they said, "That looks like fun, Lord Tokinada!"

Tokinada smiled back at Hikone as he slowly thrust his zanpaku-to into the assassin's spinal cord. "Yes, it is quite fun. Trampling on a person is fun. It's easy to grow tired of it, but after a short time you crave it again."

Tokinada spent several hours making sure all of the assassins were dead before wiping the blood off his zanpaku-to and speaking to Hikone. "Now then, let's go, Hikone. I must go announce to the Seireitei that my grand uncle has been murdered by thugs and that I have succeeded him as the head of the Tsunayashiro family."

"Yes, Lord Tokinada! Or should I call you Lord Tsunayashiro now?"

"Don't worry about that. Between you and me, Tokinada is fine."

"Really, Lord Tokinada?!"

Hikone's innocent smile glowed among the dozen or so scattered corpses. Tokinada patted the child on the head as a malicious smile spread across his face. "Why would I mind? After all, you're going to become the Soul King, Hikone, so we should treat each other as equals."

CHAPTER TWO

SEVERAL DAYS LATER,
IN THE RUKONGAI

SHUHEI HISAGI WAS A MAN OF MANY HATS. One of his occupations was Ninth Company assistant captain, which everyone knew about. His other role was editor-in-chief of the *Seireitei Bulletin*.

The *Seireitei Bulletin* was a dispatch published by Ninth Company and circulated all over the Seireitei and even occasionally to certain parts of the Rukongai. Although working on the *Bulletin* was officially considered the same as any other posting, it was so different from a Soul Reaper's regular duties that the world at large unofficially recognized it as a side business.

Until a few centuries ago, the *Seireitei Bulletin* had been little more than a simple one-page publication printed off a wooden block like the proclamations from the Edo period. But after Kaname Tosen became captain, the *Bulletin* adopted more modern printing methods from the world of the living, and it had quickly evolved.

Tosen had served as the editor himself, possibly because of his deep sincerity. Under the captain's leadership, the *Bulletin* had become a comprehensive newsletter disseminated across the Seireitei, running articles, essays, and serialized novels written directly by the captains. With Tosen no longer in the Soul Society, his assistant captain had taken over.

Customarily the new captain, Kensei Muguruma, should have become the next editor-in-chief. But Muguruma himself had said, "Back in my time, I left everything to the company soldiers. To be honest, it's not my thing," and had left it all to Hisagi. So Hisagi had forged ahead with his new position.

"So? What's brought you all the way out here, Mr. Editor-in-chief?" A puzzled woman's voice rang out from the doorway of the residence. It was none other than the leading fireworks expert of the Rukongai, Kukaku Shiba.

"I'm covering a story, of course."

"About what? Is this about the new statues? You got me. And I can tell you that those things aren't just for show." She proudly turned her eyes to the stone flagbearers Hisagi had just passed under. The two gigantic statues were both of an oddly posed, gruff man. They stood side by side, holding aloft a horizontal banner that read "Welcome to Kukaku Shiba's Residence."

"Um...Well, they're definitely a hot topic in some circles."

"If you want, you can make them the cover of the next *Sereitei Bulletin*."

"Well...I'll mention that at our planning meeting."

After that noncommittal reply, Hisagi eased into the topic at hand to get her off the subject. "Ms. Kukaku, I came here to ask for your help on a retrospective of the Great Soul King Protection War."

"What? You're doing a retrospective already? But it hasn't even been half a year!"

"That's exactly why I want to collect accurate accounts right now."

Kukaku Shiba was a fireworks technician through and through. She openly called her engagements with Squad Zero a "side hustle." As Ninth Company assistant captain, Hisagi technically outranked her. But there was an enigmatic quality about Kukaku that made most of the assistant captains treat her with deference.

Although the Shiba name had been dragged through the mud over the centuries, they had produced many high-ranking members of the Court Guard and had even once been one of the Five Great Noble Clans, alongside the Kuchiki and Shihoin. And Kukaku Shiba was nothing to scoff at herself.

Hisagi had heard that she had once taken on a sturdy Seireitei guard with nothing but kido. To Hisagi, she wasn't a mere maker of fireworks. She was a Soul Society authority of untold power.

He was there to see her for exactly the reason he had stated. Although publication difficulties had forced the *Seireitei Bulletin* to go on hiatus, they had released a small run of special issues to spread the word that they would be launching a full revival now that the war was over. Hisagi had been hoping to build the groundwork of his endeavor slowly, with the goal of formally relaunching the *Bulletin* on the anniversary of the end of the war.

After the exciting relaunch announcement, his *Teach me, Mr. Shuhei!!* column had received numerous reader requests for details about the Great Soul King Protection War. *Teach me, Mr. Shuhei!!* was a periodic column where Hisagi replied to reader questions. It was only sporadically popular, so while it was revived when there was demand, its future was unpredictable because it could be discontinued again after only few issues.

But the people of the Seireitei still didn't have a full picture of the war, and there was a deep unease about whether it was actually over and worry that something similar could happen again. They looked to the *Seireitei Bulletin* to wipe away those fears.

Many wanted the war to be the focus of the entire newsletter, but Hisagi had decided to handle all the demands in his own column. It was an important responsibility for the *Seireitei Bulletin*, and he couldn't trust it to just any old member of the company. Hisagi had decided to take the lead on the reporting and treat this as a revival of his *Teach me, Mr. Shuhei!!* column for the first issue of the restored *Seireitei Bulletin*.

Motivated by eagerness, Hisagi spent his days chasing down interviews with the Surveillance Department, the Department of Research and Development, and the special relief groups from the Fourth Company. But he hadn't been able to gather the sort of material he had hoped for.

It was unlikely that one single person had seen the full scope of the entire war. He had no idea how many accounts he would need to collect before he was able to see it himself. Doubt assailed him.

Yhwach, the person with the most comprehensive view of the war, had already been put in the ground by Ichigo Kurosaki. All Hisagi could do was gather the fragments. People wanted as much information as they could get as an antidote to the uncertain times they found themselves in. If he was able to publish the outcomes of the many battles the Soul Reapers had fought all over the Soul Society, it might bring hope to those facing the current battle—recovery.

In other words, I'm the only one who can fight this battle!

After Hisagi had spiritedly explained his mission, Kukaku crossed her arms and replied, "I know this isn't what you want to hear when you've got a glitter like that in your scary intense eyes, but I don't really have much to tell you. All I did was launch Squad Zero and Ichigo." Though her words were rough, her tone was oddly compassionate.

It made Hisagi think, *Oh, she probably really doesn't have much to say then.* She seemed to him less like someone who didn't want to talk about the past and more like someone who had gotten the job done and accepted it as routine.

"Well, I just came by to get the ball rolling. I'll come back another time."

"Coming back will just be a pain for you, and it's kind of weird for me to be commenting on Soul Reapers and your fights. So if you're going to talk to anyone, talk to my brother Ganju. He went with Ichigo and those guys to the Reiokyu, so I'm sure he's got something to say about it."

"Huh?! He went to the Reiokyu?"

Ganju Shiba had been one of the people who had appeared as a ryoka with Ichigo during the disturbance at Rukia Kuchiki's execution. It was the first time Hisagi had heard that someone from the Rukongai had gone all the way to the Reiokyu since he had withdrawn from the front during the war's endgame.

Come to think of it, I still haven't interviewed the people close to Kurosaki.

Obviously he should have interviewed Ichigo and the others who had been most deeply involved in the war's conclusion. But as inhabitants of the world of the living, they weren't part of the Soul Society. He would need to get permission from the Captain General to go all the way there to interview them.

I think I'd be able to get the Captain General's permission, but I don't know if Kurosaki will cooperate. He doesn't seem like the type to open up about himself.

If it came down to it, Hisagi wondered if he could speak with the people who were close to Ichigo instead, like Inoue or Sado. He decided to leave the Shiba residence for now.

"I see. I'll try talking to your brother first."

"Right. Ganju's probably still hanging out in West Rukongai on that boar. If you have a look around, you'll probably find him. He's an obnoxious idiot, so you'll know who he is the moment you see him."

"Yes, I saw him a few times during disturbances in the Seireitei, so I should be able to recognize him." Armed with this dynamic advice for identifying his quarry, Hisagi gave Kukaku a bow and turned his back on the house and its attached firework launcher.

Hisagi headed down the road toward where he had left his ride, which he'd gone out of his way to bring over from the world of the living and transform into reishi. But once he got close, he noticed several men gathered around it. The men had dense spiritual pressure that made them unlikely to be from the Rukongai, but they didn't feel like Soul Reapers or Quincies either.

"What's a Kawasaki Z2 doing here?" A man with slicked-back shoulder-length hair asked.

The tall young man next to him shrugged. "Who knows?"

The motorcycle from the world of the living, with its characteristic red paint, gleamed in front of them. The two men, who had died and come to the Rukongai, had gotten used to the ambient culture feeling like it was stuck around the Heian or Edo era. Many aspects of life there, from clothing to buildings, seemed to be from those far off times, possibly because the Soul Society had never experienced the social reforms that had rocked the world of the living. They hadn't seen an automobile of any sort since the moment they had arrived.

A gentleman wearing a black patch over his right eye looked at the motorcycle with deep curiosity from his position behind the other two. "Hm... Even we Fullbringers can only transfer that which is more or less a part of our bodies, like our clothes or tools, and we manipulate the souls of objects! Perhaps someone loved their motorcycle so much it became an extension of their self."

"What about gas?"

"Yes, the Soul Society doesn't really produce petroleum. Apparently most fuels go to the Department of Research and Development or to the aristocrats."

"Does that mean this motorcycle is some aristocrat's toy?"

The gentleman's face clouded at the young man's mention of that facet of the Soul Society, but a shout from behind him contradicted those assumptions. "I saved up to buy that thing! Although I guess you could call it a toy since that's pretty much what it is."

The man with slicked-back hair narrowed his eyes as he turned to face the interloper. "Oh. When the sound of a rare motorcycle lured me over, I had no idea I was about to come face to face with a Soul Reaper."

Hisagi scowled when he saw the stranger's face, which matched a description that had recently circulated several times among the Thirteen Court Guard Companies —the face of a dangerous Reaper killer, Kugo Ginjo.

Kugo Ginjo had been the first-ever deputy Soul Reaper, but he had become estranged from the Soul Society and had pursued and slaughtered countless Soul Reapers. Hisagi had never seen it for himself, but after Ichigo had killed him, the corpse of the outlaw Kugo Ginjo had remained for a time in the Soul Society. Although he had eventually been buried in the world of the living at Ichigo Kurosaki's request, his konpaku was another matter entirely. Because he had been a human of the world of the living, when his konpaku had broken free of his remains it had most likely drifted until it reached the Rukongai.

"Oh, what an honor. I can't believe someone with an assistant captain's armband recognized little old me."

Hisagi's shihakusho had no sleeves to hold his rank insignia, but he always fastened it to the wraps around his arm when he went out in public. Hisagi's voice lowered when he heard Ginjo's brazen laughter at the armband. "I heard rumors that you hadn't gone to hell, but what are you doing here?"

"Ah, that's no way to look at a stranger, is it? Did I do something to you?"

"So you're playing dumb. I haven't forgotten what you did to us Soul Reapers or to Kurosaki." Hisagi glared at the former deputy Soul Reaper with narrowed eyes.

Ginjo narrowed his eyes in reply and shot a shameless grin toward Hisagi. "And so what? You tellin' me to bow down and apologize? Listen, even though I'm in Ichigo Kurosaki's debt, I'm still not buddies with you Soul Reapers and I don't regret turning against you."

"You lowlife! What're you scheming?"

"Hah. Do I look like I'm scheming? And even if I was, what're you going to do about it?" Ginjo snorted as the tall young man next to him closed the book he was holding and removed a bookmark from its pages.

"Stand down, Tsukishima."

"Are you sure? He looks like he might try to kill you," Shukuro Tsukishima said in an unruffled tone.

At that name, Hisagi drew up his guard even more. "Tsukishima... Aren't you the guy who screwed with Kurosaki's past?"

The very same Tsukishima smiled cynically as he looked at Hisagi. "What a terrible thing to say. It wasn't *his* past I changed. Oh, I guess I did help with his sword another time."

Unable to understand Tsukishima's meaning, Hisagi gave the man a puzzled look.

The gentleman in the eye patch who observed them sighed as he said, "Mr. Ginjo, it seems he is not aware that you were one of Ichigo Kurosaki's reinforcements."

"You were a reinforcement?" *Wait, I think Abarai mentioned something about an "unexpected helping hand."* Tch. *I should've interviewed him first.*

For the past half a year, Hisagi had been working himself to the bone as the Ninth Company's acting captain while the corpseified actual captain had been undergoing medical treatment. As a result, Hisagi hadn't been able to conduct any detailed interviews while Captain Muguruma recovered.

Ignoring Hisagi, who was deeply regretting postponing interviews with the Court Guard on the assumption that he could do them anytime, Ginjo's response to the gentleman in the eyepatch seemed jaded. "I wouldn't call us reinforcements. We were just returning a favor."

Hisagi fell into thought as the leisurely conversation between the three men continued. *Can I win against these guys, one on three? I don't know who the guy with the eye patch is, but he's probably one of Ginjo's buddies. I don't*

know his abilities. I've heard about the other guy's abilities
from Madarame and Captain Hitsugaya, though...

Was this the guy who, as rumor had it, "croaked after a single swing of Kenpachi Zaraki's sword"? Hisagi considered that information, but he wasn't foolish enough to write the man off as weak just because Kenpachi Zaraki beat him with one sword stroke. Hisagi was well aware that there wasn't much difference between a wolf and a puppy in the face of someone like Kenpachi.

In any case, these men had been enemies who had slaughtered other members of the Thirteen Court Guard Companies. Ichigo Kurosaki seemed to have found a way to forgive them, but that was a separate conversation. As a Soul Reaper, he could by no means ignore their presence.

Coming to that determination, Hisagi decided that he first needed to discover their objective. He tightened his guard as he jumped back into the conversation. "Why did you betray the Soul Reapers? Why did you betray Ukitake?"

The darkness in the back of Ginjo's eyes brightened instantly. He looked surprised and exasperated. "What a surprise! Why would a Soul Reaper ask me that *now*?"

"I heard that Captain Ukitake used your deputy badge to keep an eye on you, and that was enough to make you decide that the entire Court Guard was your enemy. No one enjoys being spied on, but all you had to do was bring it up with Ukitake as soon as you discovered it."

"I should've brought it up as soon as I discovered it?" Ginjo muttered, then fell silent for a moment. Finally he laughed out loud as though he had seen some ridiculous clown act. "Hah...is that it? You don't seem like you're playing dumb, which means that even someone at the rank of assistant captain doesn't know what happened."

"What are you talking about?"

"I'm saying I really get it now—you just don't know anything!" Then his smile vanished, and he started to fidget with a cross necklace hanging around his neck.

Hisagi felt the reverberation of some sort of unpleasant spiritual pressure coming from that necklace and took a step back, reaching for his zanpaku-to. The air around them filled with the foreboding of a coming eruption, and they were quick to put distance between each other. But the tension was suddenly shattered by a rumble and the braying of a beast.

They turned to face the braying, and a gigantic boar the size of a small car came charging at them from the direction of the nearby village. It thrust itself between Hisagi and Ginjo as they faced off, slowing abruptly as it got to them. As a result, the man on its back plunged headfirst into the grass between them.

"Bwaghh?!"

The boar rider shrieked comically as he crashed into the ground, then staggered to his feet and gave a thumbs-up to the boar. "Heh, you're as enthusiastic as always, Bonnie!"

As though ignoring him, the boar raced off like the wind to a different horizon.

Hisagi's eyes went wide at the sudden, comedic exchange. The man, who had watched the boar rush off, turned to him and started talking in a voice full of authority. "Whoa, whoa, whoa! What's going on here! You havin' a fight?"

"It's nothing, Ganju. I was just riling up a Soul Reaper who hasn't got a clue how the world works."

The rough-faced Ganju looked exasperated as he continued. "You were fighting with a Soul Reaper? Seriously, I get that you hate them, but don't go around digging up trouble! I'm not gonna tell you to let bygones be bygones, but it ain't smart picking fights with them face to face."

The gentleman with the eye patch, who had been listening in, tilted his head as he asked, "What was that you said? According to Madame Kukaku, your meeting with Mr. Kurosaki was like a child's squabble."

"Guh...! I can't believe my sister's been talkin' about that!" The man, whose face was the spitting image of the flagbearing statues Hisagi had just seen, scowled as he spoke.

He was unmistakably just the man Hisagi had been looking for. But with Ganju Shiba right in front of him, Hisagi knit his eyebrows together as though troubled. "I don't know if this is good timing or what, but..."

"Hunh?! Who're you? Actually, aren't you assistant captain of whatever company...? Assistant captain Hi...Hisa..."

After an awkward pause, Ganju nodded firmly and smiled at Hisagi with the same thumbs-up he had given the boar. "Hi-sa-a-ay, it's so great to see you again! Rukia Kuchiki's assistant captain buddy!"

"C'mon, it's just one more syllable! It's Hisa*gi*! From the Ninth Company! Shuhei Hisagi!"

Ginjo sighed from where he stood next to the yelling Hisagi as he pulled his fingers from his necklace. "What? You know each other?"

Confirming that the incredibly strained atmosphere had truly eased, Tsukishima opened his book once again and dropped his eyes to its pages.

"Hey, Ganju Shiba, what's going on here? Who are these guys, and do you and Ms. Kukaku know them?"

"Of course we do! We don't just *know* them—they're freeloaders my sister picked up."

"Freeloaders...?"

Ignoring Hisagi, who had no idea what was going on, Ginjo and the two others tried to take off. But Ganju quickly spotted them and halted them with a cryptic, glowering look. "Hey, hey, where do you think you're going?! I dunno what happened between you and the assistant cap here, but I'm not gonna let there be grudges between the Soul Reapers and the Shiba gang while I'm alive!"

Ganju, unlike Ginjo and the other two men who turned around with annoyance, or the befuddled Hisagi, was full of self-confidence as he resoundingly explained the peace plan. "I won't assume anybody's in the wrong here. Just leave things up to ol' Ganju—the self-proclaimed deep-red bullet of West Rukongai! The self-proclaimed but universally acknowledged boss of West Rukongai—voted number one for fourteen consecutive years in a row! And!! The self-proclaimed former number-one Soul Reaper hater of West Rukongai, Ganju!"

Ganju beat his own drum very loudly. Ginjo and the other two men were already acquainted with Ganju but had no idea how to respond to the cryptic names he had bestowed upon himself. Hisagi looked on unimpressed and barely managed to utter something coherent. "About that last bit...? Why are you still calling yourself that if it is *former*...?"

Suddenly, his many years of experience as a Soul Reaper set alarm bells ringing in his mind. *This seems bad. I feel like I've been caught up in something that's gonna mean trouble...*

≡

SEVERAL HOURS LATER, SEIREITEI FIRST COMPANY BARRACKS

"This is definitely going to mean trouble—a lot of it."

The two assistant captains in front of Captain General Kyoraku—Nanao Ise and Genshiro Okikiba—traded quick looks at his words. Kyoraku had said the phrase half out of habit, but as assistant captains, Nanao and Okikiba knew by his voice that it was serious. Though it was something only those familiar with the Captain General could have noticed, his tone indicated that something truly terrible had happened.

"What is, Captain General?"

Kyoraku let out a long sigh at Nanao's words. "Ah, sorry, sorry. Did I worry you? Why don't you leap into my arms and let me quell your frightened shivers."

"I'm being serious, Captain General."

"Right, well. Just before you showed up, little Nayura came to me with a few guards. They had a formal message and request from the Central 46."

"You mean Nayura Amakado came here directly?" Even Nanao knew about Nayura.

The Central 46 was the acting voice of the Soul King and so led the Soul Reapers. Occasionally they acted as the supreme judiciary body and meted out judgments. Nayura Amakado was the youngest member of that body—a girl who appeared to be just ten years old. But both Kyoraku and Nanao recognized that the girl had a sharpness that came from living many years longer than her looks suggested, and that she had initiated steady changes in the Central 46, which had on principle previously served the aristocrats foremost.

As the result of Nayura and Kyoraku's efforts, the gaps in knowledge between the Soul Reapers and Central 46 had slowly been shored up. At least, that was how Nanao felt. And although the issue of balance still remained, Nanao had hopes that the differences in judicial treatment between the nobles and the Soul Reapers, or perhaps even between them and all the inhabitants of the Rukongai, was beginning to settle in a good direction.

Nanao did wish Kyoraku wouldn't use the names of the Central 46 members so casually when he spoke. But Nanao often accompanied Nayura Amakado when she occasionally observed the populace incognito, and even Nanao was close to using just her first name.

Kyoraku's face held a slight shadow as he sighed. "There was a pretty concerning incident with the four noble families earlier. I think you've heard about that."

"Yes. You're referring to the assassins who snuck into the Tsunayashiro household and murdered the head of the family?"

In peacetime, the brutal murder of one of the heads of the Four Great Noble Clans would have been enough to shake the Seireitei itself. But since the chaos of the war had yet to subside, the official public declaration was that the noble had "fallen ill from distress during the battles and passed away due to an epidemic."

That was precisely why the particulars of the incident had only been relayed to the highest ranks. Among the

Thirteen Court Guard Companies, only Captain General Kyoraku, his adjutants, and the captain of the secret remote company, Soi Fon, had knowledge of the progression of the events. "Well, Captain Kurotsuchi and Yoruichi have probably found out by their own methods. They probably even found out what happened next before I did."

"Does that mean there's a problem with who will succeed the head of the family?"

"Little Nayura gave me some general details, but issues with the nobles are out of our jurisdiction. The Gilded Seal Aristocratic Assembly deals with that, not the Thirteen Court Guard Companies. At least, for the time being..."

Nanao picked up on Kyoraku's implication and narrowed her eyes. "When you say it's theirs to deal with *for the time being*, do you mean that the situation will involve the Court Guard later?"

"Well, it'd be nice if it didn't." After letting some of his misgivings show on his face, Kyoraku looked at the official directive from Central 46 and continued, "Oh, and could you call Muguruma and Hisagi in for me?"

"From the Ninth Company?"

"Hisagi alone will be just fine. I'd like to make sure the captain knows what's going on, the situation being what it is."

≡

AT THE SAME TIME,
KUKAKU SHIBA'S RESIDENCE

"So then, just when I'm thinking that suddenly the statues weren't appearing anymore, that jerk Ichigo pops up behind us outta nowhere! And he was like 'Sorry, I ended up going down first, so I came by to get you'! Even though Chad and me were all revved up about clearing the path for Ichigo's way back! What's up with him already going back down to the Seireitei?!"

They were in the underground parlor of the Shiba residence, and Ganju was complaining to Hisagi as he slugged down his drink. "And ya know what?! That Chad guy was all, 'Ichigo can only see the path he's on'! But I sure never thought that'd *literally* be true, damn it!"

"Uh-huh...well, seems like you had a tough time."

"And that Chad guy being Chad and all! The first thing he says in that whole mood is 'I see...so it's over,' and he had a smile on his face! He made me look like a shallow dingus with how I started off by just complaining—*guh-huh*?!"

Ganju was interrupted by a kick in the back that sent him to the floor face-first. Kukaku, the one who had kicked him, stepped on her younger brother's back as she said, "Stop babbling like a baby! You haven't actually got any grit anyway!"

"But, sis! That hurt *and* was cruel!"

"No *buts*! You punk... You trained yourself for years so you could battle on the front lines till the end, so how'd you end up off the track and lost...?"

"Who told you I got lost?! It must have been Ichigo, that little *ow ow ow ow*! Will you please stop, sis?! You're gonna pulverize my back! Into smithereens!" Ganju yelled as Kukaku continued to step on her younger brother without mercy.

Not knowing how to react to the two siblings, Hisagi seemed troubled as he sipped his drink. In the midst of that ordeal, he turned his eyes toward Ginjo, who sat on his periphery.

Hisagi had been forcibly invited into the parlor earlier by Ganju in order to "let bygones be bygones by drinking together." But when he had tried to ask about the relationship between the Fullbringers and Ganju, just to have something to say, he had wound up in the plight of having to listen to Ganju's drunken complaints.

Tsukishima, incidentally, wasn't taking part in the drinking party and was instead leaning against a wall in a corner reading a book. On the way to the parlor, Giriko Kutsuzawa, the man with the eye patch, had said, "I'll fix some snacks," before withdrawing into the Shibas' kitchen.

"Actually, what's up with Tsukishima and Ginjo getting past us to Ichigo?! Isn't that kind of unfair?! Hey, isn't that unfair?!"

Ganju, who had been released from under his sister's foot, aimed his complaints at Ginjo instead. Ginjo let Ganju's words slide past him with a cool expression as he shrugged and gracefully drank. "Yukio and Riruka transported us there directly. We were crossing a pretty dangerous bridge too, you know?"

"Yukio and Riruka?"

Ginjo turned his eyes away at Hisagi's muttered question. Then Ginjo said, "Yeah, they were part of the group we hung out with in the world of the living. They're still alive, unlike us, but they still came all the way here just to help out Kurosaki."

"They came here to help him...?" As the editor of the *Seireitei Bulletin*, Hisagi wanted to pry for details, but he just couldn't bring himself to do so because of the wariness he felt toward Ginjo.

Kukaku, who saw Hisagi's hesitation, spoke out. "Don't look so miserable while you're drinking. I told you earlier, didn't I? Ganju and I have accepted these freeloaders. We haven't got any concerns about them stabbing us in the back or anything."

"But they're—!"

"We even ran it by Ukitake."

"Huh...?"

As Hisagi swallowed back his protest, Kukaku continued. "Well, it's not like we can prove that now though."

"Wait a second. Then did Ginjo meet Ukitake too?"

When Hisagi looked at Ginjo, the Fullbringer was rolling his empty cup around in his hands. "I didn't see him myself. To be honest, I was going out of my way not to see him here."

"You're saying it's different now?"

"Who knows. Suppose we had met. It might've become a battle to the death."

"Why are you so intense about him...?"

What in the world had happened between Ginjo, the first deputy Soul Reaper, and Ukitake? At the very least, Hisagi couldn't let his guard down until he knew. No—no matter what was behind the rift, nothing would change the fact that the man in front of him was an enemy and Reaper killer. *But...* Hisagi felt a slight hesitation—or perhaps it was fear he felt in his chest.

If they crossed swords now and he managed to kill Ginjo, could he honestly say that he was just fulfilling his duties as part of the Court Guard by killing an enemy of the Soul Reapers? Wasn't it wrong to let emotions swing his sword when he himself had tried to stop Captain Tosen's revenge?

Aizen's words from half a year ago came back to him. *"What you have isn't hate. All you have is sentimentality for Kaname Tosen and what he left behind after he disappeared."*

There might be some truth in that. If someone asked whether there was even a sliver of emotion in his blade, he probably wouldn't be able to deny it. But he also couldn't just overlook Ginjo. Losing sight of how to use his sword because he had been swayed by Aizen's words would be an utter failing on his part.

Acknowledging his hesitation and fear allowed him to regain his composure. He wiped the emotion from his face and, as a member of the Thirteen Court Guard Companies questioning an enemy of the Seireitei, he turned back to Kugo Ginjo.

"You're right that I don't know anything. That's exactly why I want you to tell me. What did the Soul Reapers...what did *we* do to you, the first deputy Soul Reaper?"

Ginjo, who had noticed Hisagi's internal debate, lifted one eyebrow in slight surprise and put his cup on the table. "I see. So you at least have the qualities of an assistant captain." He paused for a moment, smiling in fascination, before slowly shaking his head. "I'm grateful that you're taking it seriously, but no matter what I say, you're still going to treat me as dangerous, aren't you? How about you go and ask your Captain General about it?"

"How's that fair? The Captain General isn't one to lie, but I'm a journalist. I need to get everyone's side of the story to be impartial."

"I never thought I'd hear a Soul Reaper call himself a journalist. Besides, it's not like all journalists are impartial."

"I'm honoring the previous editor-in-chief's policy of putting fairness first."

Ginjo chuckled at his words. "You're a weird one. At first glance, you look just like a Soul Reaper, through and through."

"I'll take that last bit as a compliment."

"So? If I tell you why I became a traitor and you don't buy it, what happens?"

"You already know. When that happens—"

Kukaku, who had been silent until then, interrupted Hisagi as he readied himself to say the next words. "I'm not getting involved in a feud between the freeloaders and the Soul Reapers, but if you're gonna fight, make sure you do it out front."

"Yes, ma'am."

"Got it. I'm not going to cause you any trouble."

Hisagi nodded obediently as Ginjo shrugged in consent.

The tense air wavered, and after a few seconds Ginjo spoke. "This'll mean that I wasn't honest with Ichigo Kurosaki."

"Huh? Oh, I kind of sensed that."

"I had Tsukishima change my past, but...in *that* past, there was a half-Soul Reaper human who tried to help remove the Fullbringers' Hollow powers... In that timeline, Tsukishima killed the half-Soul Reaper and all our friends."

Every Fullbringer shared in common the fact that their parents had been attacked by Hollows. Hisagi had heard that it caused Hollow powers to course through them when they were born and to manifest as unique abilities called Fullbrings.

"So if you want to know what happened in that original past...there was never a half-Soul Reaper like Kurosaki. I was the only deputy Soul Reaper. So in that case, who killed my friends in my memory?"

"Wait a second. Aren't they part of the past that Tsukishima altered...?"

"Tsukishima's ability, the Book of the End, can stick Tsukishima into other people's pasts. He can place memories and events relating to himself into other people's histories, but he can't just conjure up someone who never existed. So the person we thought was a half-Soul Reaper was actually just one of the Soul Reapers I killed after I went into a rage."

"It couldn't be..." Hisagi gulped, getting a bad feeling.

In the corner of the room, Tsukishima had taken his eyes off his book and was watching Hisagi and Ginjo. Ganju must have gathered that it wasn't the time to interject and was listening to their conversation in silence. The look on Kukaku's face said that everything was irrelevant to her, but she quietly drank from her cup, unlike her usual self.

An unpleasant silence reigned over the parlor. Ginjo's words were the first thing to break it as he spoke with darkened eyes. "Soul Reapers killed my friends from my other past. But I don't even know what they looked like."

Silence and a cold atmosphere once again tried to fill the parlor. Hisagi stood up and shook his head to keep from being swallowed by the dark mood. "Wait...Are you saying that Ukitake told them to do that?!"

"Who knows. But that was when I figured out the secret of the deputy badge. You get what happened next without me telling you, right?"

"Uh..." Hisagi recalled their earlier conversation.

"All you had to do was bring it up to Ukitake the second you discovered it."

He hadn't known the circumstances, but when he realized how far off his words had been, he was hit with a wave of shame. "I see... I can't believe yet that this is the whole truth, but...sorry about earlier."

"Don't worry about it. It gave me a laugh."

After that little burst of humor, Ginjo continued. "I meant to meet Ukitake that day in the Reiokyu when I paid back my debt to Kurosaki. I wanted to know how much of it had been his orders. I didn't care that he hadn't trusted me from the start or that he tried to kill me, but I wanted to know why he'd killed my Fullbringer friends. It's all laughable now. I was prepared for the worst as I searched for Ukitake. I thought we'd die on each other's swords. But he couldn't even talk anymore."

"That's..." Hisagi tried to say something, but the words just wouldn't come out.

He thought of the moment Aizen had killed Tosen. Tosen had certainly been able to talk to Hisagi in the end. But Aizen had butchered Tosen before Hisagi could see whether their paths would meet again, and Hisagi had forever lost his chance to hear from Tosen again.

Ginjo clucked his tongue at the expression the memory brought to Hisagi's face and sighed. "Tch... I've said too much. I guess I let the alcohol get to me."

"Wait a second. If that's true then—" The ring of the soul pager in his pocket interrupted him in the middle of his sentence. He saw a familiar summons notification when he pulled it out to check.

"Sorry. I've been summoned by First Company."

"Speak of the devil. I wonder if the top brass is watching you too."

Hisagi replied to Ginjo's biting sarcasm. "I might believe that if it were coming from Captain Kurotsuchi instead of the Captain General. But whether or not they're watching me, I'm going to finish my work."

Hisagi stood and told Ginjo, "I can't just take your word on this. I'm a Soul Reaper too. I don't want to believe that my colleagues massacred people in the world of the living for no reason. I'll look into what's going on behind the scenes in the Court Guard. Even though I'm a Soul Reaper, I'm still the *Seireitei Bulletin* editor-in-chief. You can trust me."

"..."

"Anyway, the conversation is still just beginning. And Ganju, I want to talk to you again. Next round is on me." Hisagi bowed to Kukaku and left the Shiba residence.

As the sound of the motorbike engine echoed off into the distance, Tsukishima, who had been quiet until that moment, turned his eyes back to his book and spoke. "How unusual. I wouldn't have expected you to bring that up to a Soul Reaper yourself, Ginjo."

"Yeah. Guess I'm losing my edge." After playing it off as a joke, Ginjo looked into the air with a serious look. "Well, he seems like an honest Soul Reaper. Like he's really meant to be in the Court Guard. I didn't know if he'd listen to what I had to say, but... Well, maybe I just wanted someone to listen to me in Ukitake's place, since the guy kicked the bucket."

Giriko appeared with some plates and said, "Oh? I just finished making snacks. Did the Soul Reaper go home already?"

"Yeah, looks like he's the punctual type. He was in a hurry."

"I see, how exceptional. The flow of time is an absolute law whether we are in the world of the living, the Rukongai, or the Seireitei. Even gods of death like the Soul Reapers follow it naturally."

Ignoring the Fullbringers and their conversation, Ganju turned to his unusually silent sister who was still drinking. "Hey, sis, what did you actually think of that?"

"How should I know? I told you, didn't I? This isn't the time for us to butt in when we're not Soul Reapers."

"I wonder if our brother knew something about it." He meant Kaien Shiba, who had been Ukitake's adjutant before the fall of the Shiba household. The circumstances of his death and the disappearance of Isshin Shiba, who had been part of a branch family, had led to the Shiba family being driven out of their noble station. But Ganju still thought of his older brother as the pride of the Shiba household.

Recalling the face of her no longer present brother, Kukaku dropped her eyes to her cup. "Who knows. Soul Reapers always look outward in order to protect the Seireitei. They might just be dense when it comes to villains the Seireitei creates itself. Look at that Aizen idiot."

≡

HALF AN HOUR LATER, FIRST COMPANY COMMAND ROOM

"Yo, you're late, Shuhei. How far out did you go?"

"Sorry, Captain. I went to get an interview with Ms. Kukaku Shiba in West Rukongai."

"Kukaku...? Oh, you mean Kaien's younger sister."

The Ninth Company captain Kensei Muguruma was already there when Hisagi entered the command room, and Kyoraku was peeking his head out of the door across the way.

"Ah, you two are here. Sorry for calling you in while you're busy."

Muguruma watched Captain General Kyoraku raise his hand in his usual manner "So? What's up, Shunsui? Did you have a particular reason for bringing in just the two of us from the Ninth?"

"Well, I suppose. It's just something that relates to the *Seireitei Bulletin*."

"Huh? Then why do you need me?" Though Muguruma was the captain of the Ninth, he was in no way involved in the editing of the periodical. He had also been in recovery until just the other day after being treated for his zombified flesh and wasn't even aware of the *Seireitei Bulletin*'s recent activities.

"So, about that. The higher-ups have something they want announced directly in the *Bulletin*. I thought I'd at least tell you about it, since you're the captain."

"They want something announced? By 'higher-ups,' do you mean Squad Zero?"

"No, the Central 46. Or the aristocrats behind the scenes, to be exact."

Kyoraku turned to Hisagi for just a moment before he continued. "Actually, the head of one of the Four Great Noble Clans is changing. It's already been brought up with the government, and he's formally the head now. But he's demanding that news of his installment be broadcast extensively across the Soul Society."

"What? So it's just the aristocracy being pigheaded as usual?" Muguruma said, peeved.

Muguruma was fully aware that he didn't get along with the nobles, Yoruichi Shihoin excepted, and because they were talking about the *Seireitei Bulletin*, he quickly lost interest in the conversation.

Hisagi, on the other hand, acted as if he hadn't noticed anything. "Huh... How much of a page will it take up? We aren't planning on publishing the first issue until next month, and we're starting with a special Great Soul King Protection War retrospective, so it will have to balance with that..."

"Apparently they want you to publish a special edition. And they want you to distribute it all the way out to the Rukongai."

"A-a special edition?! Even if I can get the whole publishing system up and running right now, we really don't have that kind of budget..."

A new head of house being installed was big news, but putting out a full issue for just Four Great Noble Clan celebrations or funerals was rare because the Soul King was the highest position in the Soul Society.

This was sudden and would require funds he hadn't accounted for. If he had to distribute it all the way to the Rukongai, there was a chance it would blow through his entire year's budget.

Hisagi groaned as he tried to think of how to scrape by on budget with additional manufacturing costs, but Kyoraku smiled and clapped a hand on his shoulder. "Don't worry. The noble family said they will take on all expenses."

"Really?!" In that case, Hisagi could use the special edition as a pretext to spread word of the *Bulletin*'s return and increase subscription numbers. Hisagi started to calculate costs in his mind with a much different aim than he had a few moments before.

But—

As though to pull him back to reality, Kyoraku's smile clouded. "And about that new head of house..."

"Huh? Is something wrong, Captain General?"

"If I told you it was Tokinada Tsunayashiro, you'd recognize the name, wouldn't you?"

Thunk. Every vessel in Hisagi's body pulsed intensely. "Tokinada...Tsunayoshiro."

Hisagi *did* know that name. In order to bring Kaname Tosen back from the wrong path he had wandered down, Hisagi had tried to look into the former captain and learn even a little bit more about him. Details of the murder of Tosen's closest friend had been appalling, particularly the fact that the husband hadn't been imprisoned or properly punished and was now living his life unencumbered.

"Wait a second. Wasn't he a member of the furthest branch of the family...?"

"He's risen in the world. Aizen slaughtered the Central 46, and we were in a mess after the war. And then the head of the Tsunayashiro family and those closest to him were assassinated one after another last week."

"Captain." Nanao, who had been quiet until then, spoke.

The assassination of the Tsunayashiro household had been put under a gag order, so although Hisagi was an assistant captain, she wasn't sure if they were allowed to tell him about it so casually.

Kyoraku stopped Nanao with his hand and continued. "I won't conjecture, but Tokinada Tsunayashiro single-handedly killed all the assassins and was promoted from the branch family in light of his accomplishment. In other words, there conveniently isn't anyone else in the main family now."

Contrary to his preface, Kyoraku had phrased his words so that anyone could figure out who he was implying to be behind the assassination and what that person's goal had been. Hisagi was no exception, and he steadily scowled as the conversation progressed.

"I know about him. I think you know this already, but he's the type to do that without batting an eye."

Hisagi wasn't the only one to be astonished at those words. Nanao and Muguruma also reacted with some surprise. Genshiro Okikiba also seemed to agree with Kyoraku, based on his deep-rooted silence.

Hisagi and Nanao were surprised because they couldn't believe those words had come from Kyoraku, who rarely spoke ill of others.

As though he had noticed their surprise, a smile full of self-derision made its way to Kyoraku's face. "I'm not a saint. There are people who even rub me the wrong way."

Then Kyoraku's smile disappeared again, and he questioned Hisagi with an earnest gaze. "So you see that I need to confer with you about Tokinada Tsunayashiro's instructions to release a special edition celebrating his installment. Hisagi... Can you do it?"

CHAPTER THREE

THE SOUL SOCIETY WAS BEING steadily plagued by unusual events, such as the atrocity in the Seireitei's aristocratic quarter. And that might have just been the beginning of it. Oddly, it had begun the day Shuhei Hisagi learned that Tokinada was taking on the role of head of the Tsunayashiro household.

Signs of the budding malevolence spread, like branches and shoots, extending into the Soul Society, the world of the living, and even Hueco Mundo.

≡

SEIREITEI, FOURTH COMPANY BARRACKS

A lone, timid Soul Reaper stood silently in front of the Fourth Company barracks. He was looking down the wide road that led to the other barracks as though very concerned about something behind him.

"What's wrong, third-seat Yamada?"

The mousy young man—Yamada Hanataro—turned toward the other fourth company members who were exiting the barracks. "Huh? Oh, sorry. It's nothing! ...I think."

"Well, that answer is the opposite of reassuring," Ogido, the cool-headed seated officer, replied.

Hanataro answered falteringly, "Assistant Captain Hisagi just headed toward the Ninth barracks with this extremely terrifying look on his face. I thought something awful must have happened..."

One could hardly imagine he was anything but a timid new recruit when he replied with such a frightened expression. But in actuality, he was one of the Fourth Company's distinguished practitioners of healing kido, or kaido. And although he was fainthearted in some ways, his genial personality made him widely trusted, and he had been elevated to the position of third seat of the Fourth Company.

Hanataro, however, believed the only reason he had been promoted to the third seat was because the original seat-holder, Yasochika Iemura, had transferred to another company. Hanataro, while still trying to fulfill his duties, battled with the pressure of feeling that under normal circumstances he never would have gotten the position.

A very large Fourth Company member reacted to Hanataro's mention of the Ninth Company's assistant captain. "You saw Hisagi like that...?"

"Hey Aoga, aren't you from the same generation as Assistant Captain Hisagi?" Ogiba asked.

"Yes, but I haven't had many opportunities to see him lately. We met each other while visiting a friend's grave about half a year ago, and the last I saw of him was in a hospital room after the war." Though Ogiba seemed the much younger of the two, Aoga spoke to him deferentially because Ogiba was a seated officer.

The other Fourth Company members nearby started talking excitedly when they heard Aoga's comment.

"So Aoga's from the same generation as Hisagi..."

"That's amazing. Didn't that era produce a ton of elite Soul Reapers?"

"Yeah, that generation has produced a lot of captain-rank Soul Reapers in the decades since Assistant Captain Hisagi, like Assistant Captain Abarai, Assistant Captain Hinamori, Assistant Captain Kira, and, of course, Captain Hitsugaya. They're legends, even in Shinoreijutsuin Academy, because of how exceptionally fast they got promoted."

"If we're talking about quick promotions, what about third-seat Yamada from our very own company?"

Hanataro bowed his head to his other company members when his name suddenly came up in conversation, even though he was their third-seat officer.

"Uh, um... ...Sorry."

"Why are you apologizing?"

"Well, compared to Hisagi and the others, I'm just an incompetent causing trouble for the Fourth Company..."

When Hanataro spoke so disparagingly of himself, despite being praised, Ogiba said with a deadpan expression, "What are you saying, third-seat Yamada? You're an elite among the elites, just as good as any of them with the same lineage and skill. They say even Kisuke Urahara acknowledged that your kaido ability was better than his."

"I genuinely feel terrible... Wait, actually I feel like I kinda always get sucked into a horrible situation whenever I get involved with Urahara..."

"By the way, there's someone who's been waiting in the visitor's room for our very own third-seat Yamada for the past half hour."

"What!? Y-you could have told me that to begin with!"

After watching Hanataro scramble into the barracks, Ogiba muttered, unconcerned, "Sorry, I misspoke. He just arrived, so he hasn't been waiting very long."

One of the exasperated company soldiers who overheard that scolded, "You would've had to tell him eventually anyway. You're as unpleasant as always, Ogiba."

"Well, I would have told him if it had been someone he couldn't keep waiting. Anyway, as far as unpleasantness goes, I think that visitor is way worse."

"Huh?"

Ogiba just shrugged, and the other soldiers cocked their heads quizzically. Aoga was the only one of the group looking at the main road Hisagi had run down just a short while ago. He seemed conflicted as he said to himself, "He had a terrifying look on his face, huh?"

Aoga remembered when Hisagi had been in a grave condition after the war and had been brought into the Fourth Company for treatment. Hisagi had been so horribly injured, it was a wonder he was still alive. He had somehow managed to briefly survive thanks to Orihime Inoue, but it had taken quite some time for him to replenish his spiritual pressure after that.

After Hisagi had regained consciousness, Aoga had asked the Soul Reaper, "Are you planning on fighting again?"

When they had reunited in front of their classmate Kanisawa's grave, Aoga had thought that Hisagi had cast his fear aside, since he had continued to fight after so many close calls.

But when Aoga saw Hisagi on the verge of death again, he realized that no matter how many times a Soul Reaper cast it aside, they could never escape fear on the front lines. Hisagi's strength came from his being prepared to keep surviving even while battling his perpetual fear. That was why Aoga had known what Hisagi would say. But he still couldn't leave the question unasked.

Hisagi had just made one remark, smiling all the while. "Why are you making a face like that when we just got through the war? Kanisawa would've given you a talking to."

The next day, Hisagi forced his discharge from the hospital in order to witness Aizen's reimprisonment. It made Aoga very concerned that the very same person had just run by with a frightful look on his face. As though half praying and half frustrated by his own powerlessness, Aoga muttered, "I hope that nothing happens to make him put his life on the line in a fight, at least until reconstruction of the Seireitei is finished."

If anything happened, Hisagi would head right toward the fight, regardless of the state of the world around him. Aoga was incredibly familiar with that aspect of Hisagi's personality.

But destiny, which had Hisagi in its grasp, was already trampling Aoga's wishes underfoot.

≡

FOURTH COMPANY BARRACKS, VISITOR'S ROOM

Kaido functionality had been put first when the Fourth barracks were built, but a room with slightly more splendor in mind had still been included in the plans. It was the visitor's room, used by the Captain General or aristocrats as needed.

However, the Fourth Company prioritized the lives of the soldiers of the Thirteen Court Guard Companies foremost and had opened the visitor's room as a temporary aid station during the war. The smell of medicine and other such things still lingered faintly in the space.

Hanataro Yamada ran into the visitor's room, accompanied by the sound of his rushed footsteps. He tripped on the edge of the doorway but used the momentum of that near tumble to bow his head and apologize. "Oh whoa... Uh...um...apologies...for the delay."

Hanataro had displayed his awkward manners before even seeing the visitor's face, but the guest did not reproach him. Instead, the visitor's sage voice filled the room, "You seem and sound just as dreary as usual. When you try to sympathize with your patients, do you allow their ailments to take root in your own heart, Hanataro?"

Hanataro felt nostalgic as he realized the voice was one he was long familiar with. His eyes went wide and he raised his head. "Uh...um...S-Seinosuke!?"

"Oh, even your face has grown dreary. I worry your patients might hang themselves after a face like that treats them." That was Seinosuke Yamada. He was also Hanataro's older brother and until a few decades ago had been the Fourth Company's assistant captain. He was currently decommissioned and had retied from the Thirteen Court Guard Companies, so his zanpaku-to was in safekeeping at the barracks.

He wasn't unemployed though. Seinosuke Yamada had withdrawn from his post as assistant captain because he had been headhunted into a new occupation, which made him an exception of exceptions. The Thirteen Court Guard Companies usually stuck any discharges into a special prison called the Maggot's Nest on principle, and had required Seinosuke to formally retire in order to leave his post.

Hanataro was puzzled specifically because he knew the new occupation his brother had been recruited into. "W-what happened? Do you have the day off? I heard you were quite busy."

"Hm. More or less. But the work is worthwhile. Those old aristocrats who don't want to die even though they're Soul Reapers come to see me incessantly. Watching such authorities floundering as they disgracefully cling to something out of fear of old age is always a pleasure."

"Uh, um...are you really sure you should be saying that? E-e-especially about the aristocrats..."

"Of course I shouldn't. It's defamation and possibly even a death penalty offense. Are you planning to tattle on me, Hanataro? If you're saying you want me to die, I suppose I'll just need to be brave and give up on life as my dear little brother wishes."

"Uhh...I-I wouldn't do that, Seinosuke..."

After waving his hands back and forth in a fluster, Hanataro awkwardly disclaimed, "Y-you certainly are spiteful, and no one's a fan of your personality, but...there are good things about you if people look for them...I think... We can't let anyone who has it out for someone join the Fourth Company to begin with!"

"It hurts me in its own way that you'd consider it so seriously." Despite his words, Seinosuke smiled as though he were enjoying himself and shrugged before he broached the subject at hand. "Well, it's my day off and I had some business here. So I came to give you some advice while I was around, Hanataro."

"Advice...for me?"

Seinosuke narrowed his eyes slightly, and his smile disappeared as he got to the crux of the conversation. "Hanataro, how would you feel about taking some time off from the Fourth Company?"

"Huh?"

"A lot of rumors come my way in my line of work."

When Hanataro seemed puzzled at the sudden request, Seinosuke, the Seireitei Shino-Seyakuin delegate—in other words, the highest authority in the relief office that specifically catered to the Four Great Noble Clans and specialized in serving the upper nobility—snickered. "Now that we've done away with the Quincy threat, it's unlikely that we'll be having any big wars for a while. Instead, the Seireitei will probably hit a rough patch. And not one that's small enough to stop just by putting some effort into it either.

"If you don't want to get dragged into the mess, you should distance yourself from positions of responsibility for a while and keep your eyes and ears closed."

≡

THE WORLD OF THE LIVING, KARAKURA TOWN

"AHHHHHHHHHHHHHHHH! I can't believe we got dragged into this! We're really deep in it this time!"

It was dusk in Karakura Town. Keigo Asano, who had been enjoying his day off just minutes earlier, was running down a deserted alley and filling the area around him with tearful shouts.

Mizuiro Kojima, the poker-faced boy running next to him, said, "You've got to be quiet, Keigo. You're wasting your energy by yelling."

"You know, I've been wondering about this for a while, but how do you always keep a cool head whenever something like this happens?"

"Because there isn't really a point in panicking, I guess." Mizuiro kept up his pace as he glanced behind him.

"I've never seen a monster like that before, but I suppose it's better than that walking pile of lies, Aizen." He was looking at a giant crab-shaped abomination, a Huge Hollow that was closing in on them, raising its claws with an unpleasant gnashing sound.

Mizuiro Kojima, Keigo, and Tatsuki Arisawa had once been pursued by Sosuke Aizen. This time as their pursuer got close, they didn't experience that feeling of death bearing down on them. That made things better than last time, but it was their only consolation. Their lives were still in danger. At least the monster wasn't directly after Keigo and Mizuiro right then.

The target the Hollow *was* trying to crush with its claws was a young man in a shihakusho running just behind Keigo and Mizuiro.

"Ahhhhhhhhh! Th-this is dangerous! It's dangerous, so leave this to me and get out of here! Also, somebody save me! Anyone!" The young Soul Reaper, wailing just about as much as Keigo, kept running away from the Hollow without even the mental composure to activate his zanpaku-to's shikai.

Ryunosuke Yuki, the Soul Reaper in charge of Karakura Town, had come across a Hollow stronger than he was and had, in the middle of running away in a panic, gotten Keigo and Mizuiro caught up in the mess as they were walking down the alley.

Keigo and Mizuiro had been swept up in many such incidents because of their friendship with Ichigo Kurosaki, and they had even received something called *soul tickets* from an eye patch-wearing Soul Reaper. All in all, they had become rather attuned to spiritual phenomena.

They had occasionally caught a glimpse of Ryunosuke and at least knew his name from Orihime and the others. But they hadn't tried to get involved in his business themselves, believing that he had to be stronger than "fro-man" if he'd been picked as that guy's successor.

But while the young Soul Reaper had replaced the man Keigo called "fro-man" and whom Ichigo referred to as "Imoyama" and whose real name was Zennosuke Kurumadani, Keigo and Mizuiro were just now realizing he was actually much less dependable than they had imagined.

When Keigo saw Ryunosuke fleeing and the unpromising way the Soul Reaper failed to even unsheathe his zanpaku-to, Keigo screamed even louder. On the other side of things, Mizuiro was serenely wondering, *Can we can get to Mr. Urahara's shop if we keep up this pace?*

Mizuiro had more or less heard about Urahara Shoten from Ichigo, who had told him it was a safe place to escape to if a Hollow ever attacked while Ichigo wasn't around. During the Aizen incident, Mizuiro had gathered what information he could and had concluded that the owner of Urahara Shoten was a big shot of captain rank or higher.

"He'll probably try to con you into buying all kinds of crap though. Well, just think of it as thanks for him saving you and go with it."

After Ichigo had told him that, Mizuiro had gone to check out the store many times when nothing bad was happening. It had indeed been stocked with dubious products like the ghost medicine rub Stiff-Be-Gone Theta and the spirit repellent Spray X, which were obviously not being sourced from normal manufacturers.

"Oh, actually!" Reminded of something, Mizuiro started to rummage dexterously through his bag as he ran.

"W-w-w-what are you doing, Mizuiro!? Are you going to pull out a stun gun again or something like that!? But I can't see a chance in hell of us holding that thing back with a stun gun!"

Mizuiro pulled a ball with a strange face drawn on it out of his bag. It was a Zeta Ball, as Mizuiro recalled. An electromagnetic capture bomb.

When he had asked the girl who looked like she should have been in middle school but who was working as the shop clerk how to use it, she had explained, "Uhh...if you're being chased by something beyond human understanding, twist the knob on the back and throw it at the Hollo...at the monster."

"Well, this is a last resort," Mizuiro muttered. He took the thing he'd been carrying around in place of a good luck charm, did as he'd been instructed, and threw it at the gigantic crab monster.

Lightning and a terrible sound engulfed them in the next second, and the monster's whole body twitched as its movements slowed.

"Whoa, that's harsh. If I'd chucked that thing at a person, they'd probably be dead."

Keigo was taken aback at Mizuiro's calm statement. He slowed down. "What was that!? A stun gun!? Uh...huh? What was that!? A stun gun!?" Keigo repeated himself, as though he'd given up thinking after the initial utterance.

Mizuiro kept Keigo in the periphery of his vision. He expected the young man in black to start going on the offense. But Ryunosuke Yuki, the essential part of that equation, had been so shocked by the recent roar and lightning that he was paralyzed with fear.

"Guess we've got to restart the marathon." Though its movements had been impaired, they hadn't completely beaten the monster. Mizuiro started to think that at this rate, they might need to grab Ryunosuke and run.

But his train of thought was abruptly derailed by a voice echoing through the alley—a girl's powerful shout!

"What do you think you're doing, Ryunosuke?"

Mizuiro saw the silhouette of a girl leap down from the roof of a building and confirmed that she was the Soul

Reaper who had come to Karakura Town with Ryunosuke. *I think her name was Shino Madarame?*

As her shihakusho billowed, Shino used her downward momentum to swing the naginata blade of her zanpako-to with as much force as she could muster. The terrific impact of the blade shook the surrounding alleys like an earthquake. The huge, crab-shaped Hollow was smashed to smithereens, and the resultant soul particles were purified by the zanpaku-to.

Keigo looked at the Soul Reaper who had defeated the gigantic monster in a single swing with surprise while Mizuiro calmly grasped the situation. *Oh, so some Soul Reapers are dependable.*

Ryunosuke, who realized that the Hollow had been purified, looked at Shino with relief and said, "So you're safe, Shino... I'm so glad."

"That's what I should be saying to you, you fool!" Shino, who had landed with her back to Ryunosuke, leapt backward immediately and crashed into him with her shoulder. Whether it was intentional or coincidental, she sent Ryunosuke tumbling to the ground as though performing a luchador's *tope en reversa* and then locked his arms and legs while he was down.

"You're pitiful! How could you freeze up during the chance of a lifetime?!"

"Ow ow ow! You're going to tear me apart! My arms are going to fall right off, Shino! You're going to break my arms and neck and back at this rate!"

Keigo let out a huge sigh as, watching the two Soul Reapers exchange what could have been dialogue in a comedy skit, he realized that they really were finally out of danger. "Whew, you saved us. It's Shino, right? I think I've seen you around before."

"Huh? Oh, you're that guy, aren't you? The one my big bro Ikkaku took under his wing when he was in the world or whatever."

"Your big bro Ikkaku?! Is that what he thinks of me?! That baldy didn't take me under his wing! He didn't do a single kind thing for me at all!"

When Ikkaku Madarame came to the world of the living, he had threatened Keigo Asano into housing him, partly against the boy's will. One of the main reasons the Soul Reaper had been allowed to stay was because Keigo's older sister had been all for it.

"I'm just going to pretend I didn't hear that... Ikkaku would kill you if he found out you called him baldy."

Once they were in a calmer location and could talk, Mizuiro and Keigo found out that Shino was probably Ikkaku Madarame's little sister or possibly his cousin. The uncertainty was because their family had been in daily violent struggles in the Rukongai, and their parents had died one after another before they had been old enough to form memories. They were then passed around to various relatives, so they themselves didn't know exactly what their relationship was to each other.

Although she had followed in Ikkaku's footsteps and attended Shinoreijutsuin after he had unexpectedly be-come a Soul Reaper, Ikkaku had told her, "I think you'll have a tough time in the eleventh company." The top brass must have come to the same conclusion, since she was currently assigned to the Thirteenth Company.

"Seriously, we've been training ever since that war with the Quincies ended, but there's no point if you wuss out right at the critical moment!"

"Ugh, I'm sorry, Shino..." Ryunosuke's shoulders slumped as Shiho chewed him out.

Possibly because he couldn't just stand by and watch Ryunosuke suffer anymore, Keigo tried to redirect the conversation in order to put an end to the lecturing. "So actually, I haven't been too concerned about it since Ichigo came back safe, but shouldn't there be fewer of those white monster things now that the fight's over?"

Shino breathed a small sigh at the question from the boy who had been dragged into their business. "It's not like we or Kurosaki were fighting against the Hollows. And Hollows are already more likely to appear here anyway..."

Mizuiro nodded as though he understood. "Right, since this is a special sacred place. Supposedly that's why Aizen targeted it."

"You sure know a lot for a human. That's right. That's why anything could happen here. So we can't ever let our guard down."

Ryunosuke spoke up with a serious look in his eye. "Well, I think that I've been *incredibly* careful since the moment we were dispatched!"

"Stop making that call for yourself!"

Ryunosuke's shrieks as Shino put him into a joint lock echoed through the streets of Karakura Town. Then, as though to extinguish his screams, a loudspeaker boomed from the main street.

"...and so, they were unsatisfied remaining in the present, yet humanity was left with no desire to return to the past, and those seeking a spiritual guide broke away to form a new world..."

"What's that?" Shino scowled when she heard a voice flowing out of what seemed to be a campaign van.

Mizuiro replied, "It's a new religious group. They formed because most of the world was in chaos after the earthquake half a year ago."

The extended earthquake had happened during the war between the Soul Reapers and Quincies, when the boundaries between the Soul Society, the world of the living, and

Hueco Mundo had almost been destroyed at the death of the Reio.

The world of the living had been hit by a gradual and deep *unease* because the monumental, protracted earthquake had been caused by something outside the known geological processes and was scientifically unexplainable.

Many people had felt a foreboding, and it could even be said that they had *sensed* something. They had experienced an incredibly powerful force that surrounded the world, a force inexplicable by science or logic.

Although it had officially been reported as "a large-scale seismic shift that, according to all collected data, was of unprecedented magnitude, the source of which is still being investigated," that hadn't been enough to clear away the disquiet in people's minds.

As a result, spiritual leaders seeking their own answers or people looking to take advantage of the fears of others had started forming new religions one after another, which gradually spread across the world in a jumbled chaos of and bad. At present, the new religions that had particular momentum had started to broadcast their doctrine using campaign vans.

To bring Mizuiro up to speed, Keigo told them what he knew with a serious look in his eye. "Apparently they're saying that their religious leaders can actually perform miracles or something. But what's most important is that there are rumors that a ton of the sect leaders are hot girls with wicked bods! There's actually a world out there where one of the hotties might come to recruit me directly! I've been waiting half a year—gotta be patient!"

Shino looked unimpressed as she asked Mizuiro, "Hey, can I punch this guy?"

"I don't see why not."

As Mizuiro nodded, Ryunosuke asked something he had been wondering about. "So what's it called again? That new religious organization?"

"Right, I'm pretty sure it's..."

≡

WORLD OF THE LIVING, THE PRESIDENT'S OFFICE OF A LARGE CORPORATION

"Thank you for allowing me the opportunity to speak to you, President Vorarlberna." The woman, who had been led into a simple room with a black color scheme, sat down on a sofa and respectfully nodded her head toward a boy playing a handheld game. She wore an alluring designer suit, and although her ensemble was pragmatic, anyone who saw her would notice the enigmatic sensuality about her.

But the boy, Yukio Hans Vorarlberna, gave her not even so much as a glance as he continued to fiddle with his game, saying in an uninterested tone, "You can skip the fake pleasantries. What do you want?"

The woman politely replied to the boy's question, "My, my. There's only one reason to meet with President Vorarlberna, spokesperson for Y-Hans Enterprises, the company destined to be the champion of the future. A young genius like you has the talent to lead the people into the future. As the guides to the righteous world that will inevitably be revealed to us, we'd like you to support our doctrine."

Y-Hans Enterprises was a colossal company in Yukio's portfolio that was currently vigorously expanding its undertakings. Yukio had usurped leadership from his father, and although he didn't care much about the company itself, he had decided that one of his current life goals was to expand it. After battling Ichigo Kurosaki and the Soul Reapers, he wanted to create a foundation for the future that would welcome other stray Fullbringers like himself. Riruka Dokugamine had joined him in the endeavor, and with things moving faster than he had anticipated, Riruka was bringing Jackie Tristan in to join them.

The young company president and secret Fullbringer asked the woman he had invited into his presidential office in a cold tone, "Do I look like somebody who'd fall for that fake intro?"

"Would you rather I go right into 'We'll help you with your expansion if you donate to our organization'?"

"That's a load of crap too. You—no, your organization—isn't looking for *donations* from me."

Yukio continued speaking indifferently, in the same tone as someone muttering to themselves while reading a book. He took a hand from his game and pulled a business card out of his breast pocket before putting it on the table. Then, seeming somewhat annoyed with the woman, he said, "This caught my eye earlier, and now that you've come to see me, I'm certain. You don't have any retries after this, so personally I think you should be honest."

The business card was the one that had been passed through from the front desk when the organization had made this appointment. Staring at the name of the organization on the card, Yukio once again asked, "What's your aim?"

The woman's name was written on the card in a simple script. And under it was a name Yukio could never overlook.

Aura Michibane
Xcution Representative

≡

HUECO MUNDO,
HALF A YEAR AFTER
THE GREAT SOUL KING PROTECTION WAR

Hueco Mundo, the world of the Arrancars and home to the Hollows, was undergoing a gradual change. After the Arrancar hunts of the Vandenreich Quincies had come to an end, the powerful Arrancars like Halibel and Grimmjow had temporarily disappeared, and Hueco Mundo had entered a new era of civil war.

But now that Nelliel, who been previously missing, had up till then, had returned with Halibel in tow, ambitious Arrancars and Vasto Lordes-level Menos Grandes had immediately been discouraged and gone back to their own colonies.

Several Arrancars had attempted to launch a surprise attack on Nelliel and Halibel in order to "get them while they're tired," but most had been beaten at their own game. And those who had run had the unlucky fate of bumping into an irritated Grimmjow.

The return of the king had gradually returned peace to Hueco Mundo, and so a man wearing a mask resembling a cow skull sighed. "It was a short-lived dream, wasn't it?"

He was Rudobon Chelute, the former Arrancar leader of the Exequias who had once been under Aizen's control and had single-handedly taken over running Las Noches after Aizen's exit.

"It truly was presumptuous of a weakling like me to have dreamed so big in the first place." He was one of the Arrancars who had attempted to unify Hueco Mundo after Halibel's disappearance. Rudobon still felt indebted to Aizen and, to the best of his ability, had been attempting to protect the new order Aizen had created when he usurped Hueco Mundo from King Barragan.

There were many Arrancars who were stronger than him, including the Tres Bestias and the Espada, and from the start they had had little interest being ruled and had never attempted to participate in the fights for the right of succession. In a way, it could be said that Rudobon had been the only one who had put *public order* foremost and fought for hegemony.

It wasn't like he didn't have ambition. He couldn't deny that his dream had been to develop Hueco Mundo someday and be recognized by Aizen as something superior, like an Espada.

He had heard that Aizen had been disappointed in the Espadas and had literally cut down Halibel, but when Aizen returned Rudobon wanted to tell the man that he had done *something* with the power he had been granted. He wanted to do that even if Aizen was disgusted by his clumsy results and killed him on the spot.

Right now, Rudobon was naturally fighting against the Quincies to protect Hueco Mundo's order.

"My, to think that there are still Quincy survivors."

After stealing Halibel's throne half a year ago, a Quincy hunter unit called the Jagd Armee had spread across Hueco Mundo, pursuing Arrancars everywhere they went.

Most of the detached Quincy forces had been stranded in Hueco Mundo after Ichigo Kurosaki beat their general hunt commander Quilge, as well as Grimmjow and the other Arrancars. They had taken on all sorts of forms as they kept up their hopeless resistance with desperate suicide attacks and guerilla warfare, but most of the Quincies had been annihilated by Rudobon and his Exequias.

There had been no Quincy movement in the several months since then, and Rudobon had thought their exterminations complete when he received word of a Quincy sighting and prepared for attack.

"How utterly cowardly. The Picaro aren't listening to me, as always, and I heard that they went off to the world of the living with Paramia Roka. And Master Grimmjow is still refusing to help repress anything in Hueco Mundo. How many days must we wait until proper order is reinstated?"

Rudobon shook his head at his own inadequacy and headed toward the area of the Quincy sighting, but someone spoke up to protest his statements. "Wait a sec! Don't just go around sighing. You've got to fight occasionally too! You're always shoving the work off onto us and the minions you created!"

"Don't push it, Loly. It's no use telling him that." Menoly Mallia, an Arrancar with cropped hair, chided the pigtailed Loly Aivirrne, the Arrancar who had just told Rudobon off.

Rudobon had taken them in when they were brought to Las Noches on the verge of death after a fight with Quilge. They had been accepted into the Exequias immediately because of their combat abilities, with the aim of helping to dismantle the Quincies. But they had refused to fall into line, possibly because they weren't under Rudobon's direct control.

"No, I'm going to say it! You know what, Rudobon?! Where were you when Lady Halibel was kidnapped? You weren't even here when that Quilge guy came!"

"Since the invasion started everywhere simultaneously, we needed someone everywhere to stop them. If you really want to talk about it, not a single one of us was there when Ichigo Kurosaki defeated Lord Aizen. We, myself included, must take our incompetence to heart."

"That has nothing to do with what I was talking about."

Rudobon sighed and shook his head at Loly as she grumbled complaints. "Though you are both immature, I allow you to stay in my unit because you respect Lord Aizen. Normally knaves like the two of you would have no place in Hueco Mundo because of the disruption you bring to the public order."

"Oh? And what exactly are you saying gets disrupted by my just being here?"

"I said quit it."

"Let go, Menoly! He acts all high and mighty, but what do you think he was doing when the Soul Reapers attacked? They say he almost croaked when he got beat up while Yammy was passing through!"

"But that happened to us too." Menoly pulled Loly away from Rudobon by the arm.

The girl, veins popping on her forehead, was still trying to have her say even as she was dragged away. But then a single ray of light passed in front of her eyes. The shot of light pierced a rock some distance from Rudobon and the girls. As though something had taken a gigantic bite out of the massive boulder, a piece of it went flying.

"What!?" Loly's eyes opened wide and she turned toward the direction the light had come from. She found a woman holding a bow standing on the upper floor of a collapsed building. The woman's clothes looked very similar to what the Quincies who had tried to capture them had worn.

There were other human-shaped figures stirring behind the woman, and it seemed like several people must be attacking them at once. Menoly saw that even more Quincy arrows had been sent flying toward them at a terrific speed.

Menoly and the others tried to dodge in a fluster. Rudobon's skeleton soldier followers got caught up in the attack, and countless columns of sand sprayed up from the Hueco Mundo desert.

Loly looked fearfully at the crater of sand that had been left behind and yelled in a cold sweat, "Wait, these guys aren't the usual nobodies! There're still Quincies like that around?!"

"Those Arrancars have nothing if not numbers. Feels like they came to take care of us," said a girl with a poker face holding a short bow that made one think of a shark tooth.

A voice responded to her from the darkness of the building half-reduced to rubble. "Actually, looks like all you've dealt with are the underlings. Did you really miss from this distance? Wow, so pathetic. I bet it's cuz you don't practice."

"Shuddup, Gigi. You could lift a finger every once in a while. This is a chance to get more pawns under your control, isn't it?"

Giselle Gewelle, the Quincy called Gigi, had a mechanical smile on her face that revealed none of her thoughts to the other girl. "You already know that I can only turn Hollows into zombies temporarily, don't you? I thought it was common sense that Hollow reishi and ours doesn't get along. Did you forget?"

"Who cares if it's only temporary? You pretty much treated everybody except Bambi like they were disposable anyway. The zombification ran its course over *there*, so it'll be the same here, right?"

"It makes me tired, so I don't want to. But if you're so insistent, why don't *you* become a zombie for me, Lil?" Gigi cocked her head at Liltotto Lamperd, but Lil remained expressionless as she turned her spite on her partner.

"You want me to eat you? No, I'd better not. You'd definitely give me the runs."

"That's so mean, Lil! Telling a girl she'd turn your stomach is such an insult. Hey, don't you agree, Bambi?" Gigi kept smiling mechanically as she turned to the girl with clay-red skin who had been placed in a corner like a doll among the debris.

The *thing* that Gigi had called Bambi—a corpse doll seemingly lacking all warmth in its head, torso, and exposed limbs—replied, "Y-yes, e-exactly like you said, Gigi... So, so please, Gigi... please...blood..."

"Really, Bambi. You're so greedy. If you're going to be so demanding... Well, you know what you need to do, right? Because you're so smart, aren't you? You're clever."

"...I-I got it...I'll defeat...the enemy... I'll...protect you...because I love...your blood..."

Bambietta Basterbine, the red corpse, staggered up. Lil seemed exasperated as she said, "It doesn't look like she's completely healed yet. And isn't her ability to speak getting worse? She's like Frankenstein's monster or some kind of a horror that accidentally made its way out of the woods and into civilization."

"She's fine. She'll fix up just fine once I give her my blood. But I think she looks so much cuter when she's hurt, so I'm going to keep her like this for a while, all right?"

"You really are scum." Although Lil was blunt in her disdain of Gigi's notions, she didn't try to stop Bambietta from heading toward the enemy. That was because Lil understood. Bambietta's mental faculties were minimal, that while as long as her abilities were working, she wouldn't have any trouble knocking around the average Arrancar or Hollow. And as though to prove that—

Innumerable clumps of reishi ejected from Bambietta and pierced the gathered enemy. The white desert was filled with brilliant explosions.

Liltotto Lamperd.

Giselle Gewelle.

Discounting Bambietta, who had been turned into a corpse doll, how were the women who should have died after rebelling against Yhwach in the Soul Society still alive and in Hueco Mundo?

To find out, we must journey back to the time immediately after the conclusion of the war between the Soul Reapers and the Quincies.

≡

HALF A YEAR AGO,
SOMEWHERE IN THE WORLD OF THE LIVING

When Lil woke, she was in an unfamiliar room. A bandage was wrapped around her torso, and a dull pain rushed through her when she touched it.

Someone must have used a specialized Quincy healing technique on her, but she hadn't made a complete recovery.

Obviously I wouldn't.

She could remember challenging Yhwach to a fight and being cut down before she could even use her abilities. Right before she had collapsed, Bazz-B's spiritual pressure had vanished from the position where he had been battling further away.

My guts were gouged out and shredded. That should have been fatal if left untreated. Why am I alive?

Lil turned to her side and saw Gigi still unconscious and what looked like Bambietta in the back, prone and wrapped all over with bandages like a mummy. All three of them had been laid down on simple cots and given the bare minimum first aid. Lil recognized that the pillow beneath her head was a provisional article from the Vandenreich and guessed that this was one of their bases in the world of the living.

I sense a lot of Quincies outside the room, but most of them probably just barely scraped by with their lives.

As Lil sat up and looked around her, the door opened and a woman poked her head in.

"Are you awake, Liltotto Lamperd?"

It was a female Quincy with dark eyes and a frigid expression.

"You're..." Lil was on her guard. "Aren't you Yhwach's lapdog? You accidentally saving your enemies now?"

Lil was referring to Jugram Haschwalth, who was basically number two in the Vandenreich and carried the Stern Ritter B. The woman who had just walked into the room was one of Haschwalth's attendants who had no Schrift, a prominent Quincy among the common soldat.

Though she was said to exceed some of the Stern Ritter in pure archery skills and battle ability, supposedly she hadn't received a Schrift because she herself preferred to remain under Haschwalth's command rather than become one of the Schrift holders who stood as equals, although not to Yhwach, of course.

Her superior, Haschwalth, had been Yhwach's retainer. This woman should have had reason to help Lil and those who had started a rebellion against the Vandenreich. "What's gotten into Haschwalth's head? We ain't givin' you nothing if you interrogate us. The only reason we betrayed Yhwach was because we were annoyed."

Haschwalth had a cautious personality, and he had probably assumed that traitors like themselves had bugs on them from the Soul Reapers or some other organization. That thought was going through Lil's head, but the female Quincy shook her head slightly.

"Lord Haschwalth passed in battle after offering his power to his majesty."

"Huh?"

Lil scowled at the unexpected news. But the explanation that followed left Liltotto Lamperd, former member of the Stern Ritter, absolutely shocked.

"His majesty also passed away in the battle between Ichigo Kurosaki, who was particularly powerful, and Sosuke Aizen."

"What!"

Unusually for Lil, her eyes grew wide and her mouth gaped open and closed several times. After a dozen or so seconds, her expression resumed its usual composure. "You serious? I knew that Kurosaki was stupid strong, but I didn't think he was that ballsy. I thought he was as naive as he was strong."

Lil remembered the orange-haired Soul Reaper who had yelled "Get out of the way, idiot!" when he had released a gigantic slashing attack, and grinned somewhat derisively at herself.

"Hey, what happened to Candy and Meni?" She meant Candice Catnip and Meninas McAllon. They were part of the group she had been working with during the war, and though it was unusual for her, she had accepted them as her friends among the Stern Ritter.

Normally she spewed vitriol at them, but apparently her relationship with them was such that she could ask about them by name directly in this sort of situation. Lil was half resigned to that fact as she waited quietly for the other Quincy's reply.

"We went to rescue them, but we didn't make it in time. They were captured by the Twelfth Company right after his majesty used Auswählen to take their Voll Stern Dich. Lord Najahkoop's status is unknown too, although we believe he was transferred as well."

"I don't give a rat's ass about that lecher NaNaNa. But wait, you said Twelfth Company. Ahh, might've been better if they'd just straight up died." Lil knew from previous information what kind of man Captain Mayuri Kurotsuchi was and what kind of department the Twelfth Company ran.

"Actually, I guess that means there's a chance they're still alive."

Lil glanced at Gigi, who slept next to her. As long as they had Gigi's Schrift Z, The Zombie, the others could be revived even if they lost some flesh to the Twelfth Company's *experiments* and *dissections*. And at worst even if they were dead, as long as their bodies and brains remained intact, they could be revived into zombies like Bambietta.

But there was nothing that could be done about the wounds to their psyches. After thinking that far, Lil asked the Quincy woman in an indifferent tone, "Back to the main point, why'd you save me?"

"It was Lord Haschwalth's will. When his majesty had his final slumber, Lord Haschwalth ordered us to collect and treat the soldats under direct command, such as you and the other wounded."

"I don't get it. What happened to the direct guard?" Though she scowled in her confusion, Lil continued seeking to gather more facts.

Lil's question was met with the female Quincy mournfully shaking her head as she said, "They all passed in battle. According to reports from the scouts, Lord Gerard's powers were fully absorbed by his majesty and disappeared."

"So even Nakk Le Vaar got done in. That'd definitely be lethal then." *Guess we just underestimated those Soul Reapers.*

Lil looked like she went about things at her own pace, but she was cool-headed enough to gather information in advance. She knew the direct guard's capabilities to a certain extent, so if those unrivaled men had been removed from the equation, she could certainly believe that Yhwach and Haschwalth had died in battle.

If they crushed even Gerard, a trusted retainer who took the Reio's heart, does that mean Yhwach really was driven into a corner? He was going on and on about being able to see the future when he got Gigi and me, but what kind of future did he see with those creepy-ass eyes?

Wait a sec...

"You said Haschwalth told you to save us when Yhwach was sleeping, right?"

"Yes. It was immediately after his majesty fell asleep."

Haschwalth was only only given the Mask of the Ruler at night while Yhwach slept, and was then able to fully exercise power in Yhwach's stead.

"So, did that Haschwalth see the future too?"

Lil asked the question almost as though speaking to herself, but the female Quincy dropped her eyes as she went on. "When he conveyed his orders to me, he mumbled, almost as though to himself, that the ability to see the future was unfair."

"What'd that jerk see? Are you saying that he saw a future where he and Yhwach were dead?"

"I cannot know." The features of the female Quincy who had been Haschwalth's most trusted retainer appeared overcome with sadness. She continued speaking with faint grief tinging her shamed voice. "Lord Haschwalth did not make clear what was on his mind. Not to we Stern Ritter, and I believe not even to his majesty. He simply said at the very end, 'No matter what happens, keep the Quincies' futures connected.'"

"So you were naive enough to save traitors like us? I'll tell you this for free: don't expect Gigi or me to feel like we're in your debt."

"I do not mind. We weren't expecting compensation. I was simply following Lord Haschwalth's orders."

Lil lightly clucked her tongue at the woman's dispassionate response and said, "Well, we survived because of you. I'll at least thank you for that. But don't expect Gigi to thank you. She might even turn you into a zombie when she wakes and try to use your flesh to heal her wounds."

"..."

"Don't look at me like that. At least I know how to take responsibility for things. I'll keep Gigi in check, and we'll leave as soon as we can move."

Haschwalth's trusted adviser left the infirmary as Lil checked on Gigi. The female Quincy had told Lil one lie. Before going into his last battle, Haschwalth had left behind other words.

"Perhaps Uryu Ishida was his majesty's last trial for me. I do not know the reason why, but he is the only one who can leave me shaken. If I am ever swayed by my emotions and forget my role as balancer, then on that occasion I will likely need to return the power I have been entrusted with and my life to his majesty." He had said it almost as though he had seen that future himself.

But if he had seen it, why hadn't he been able to avoid it? If he hadn't been able to hold back his emotions even though he knew the future, then what did Uryu Ishida say, or perhaps what had he *done* to Haschwalth?

At this point she just didn't know anything, and as his trusted retainer she could only be proud of her master. Even if he had seen his own future, he had been fully prepared for it, and she believed he had chosen that path for himself.

Liltotto, Giselle, and Bambietta disappeared the following day from the base hidden in the world of the living.

≡

And now Liltotto and her two companions were fighting the Arrancars in Hueco Mundo.

Although it had taken several months for them to regain their strength, they had finally recovered all their abilities, other than the Voll Stern Dichs that Yhwach had stolen from them.

"If we could just go into Voll Stern Dich, we could absorb all their reishi."

A Voll Stern Dich was a Quincy's final form. As long as they had the Sklave Rai ability from their heiligenschein halo, they could decompose all the reishi around them and force the particles to submit to them. Even Hollow reishi, which was naturally poisonous to Quincies, could be fully decomposed and therefore absorbed by Quincies without

harm. But there were no longer any Quincies with
that power.

Uryu Ishida and his father, who had escaped from
Yhwach's Auswählen, might have been able to do it. But
when Lil thought about how much use it was to her if her
enemies had that power, she just shrugged.

Gigi spoke up from behind her. "Huh? But can't you
practically do the same thing, Lil? You could just swallow
all those guys whole. Or are you on a diet?"

"It's not like I *can't* eat them, but poison is still poison.
I'd get horrible heartburn, so no thanks," Lil answered
without interest as she watched Bambietta overrun them.

Gigi kept speaking. "In the end most of them got done
in, didn't they? The survivors of the Jagd Armee, I mean."

"Every single one of them was pitiful. Even after
marching through this boring desert for two whole
months, we haven't found a single one worth anything
in a fight."

The girls were presently taking it upon themselves
to rescue independent units of Quincies to find people
they could force into being their pawns. Their ultimate
goal was to launch a surprise attack on the Soul Society's
Twelve Company and rescue Candy and Meni.

"You could just leave them there, but you sure do value
friendship sometimes, don't you, Lil? Plus I bet part of
why you're rescuing the dregs of the Jagd Armee is to

repay that infirmary for their kindness instead of making them into your pawns, right?"

"Who knows. I'm just forcing those guys to deal with ones who'll slow me down."

"It's really gross when your chilly features look all passionate like that, but I also totally like it."

"Could you just choose between praising me or bad-mouthing me, you dirty tramp?" Lil spoke dispassionately and without expression.

For some reason Gigi smiled as though she were kind of happy about being called a tramp. She answered as though enjoying herself, "Oh you got me, it's all a lie. You're so cute when you're embarrassed, Lil. It's not like we can just leave them there like that. And if Candy and Meni are dead, I can make them my zombies."

Gigi's happy expression disappeared as a certain man's face came to mind, and her voice filled with resentment. "And I just won't feel right until I give that bedazzled pervert hell."

"Don't. That guy completely outclasses us."

Gigi continued even though Lil had scolded her. "We'll be fine as long as we're using our heads. Like, what if we turn Ichigo Kurosaki into a zombie?"

"I'd really rather you not do that, specifically. I'm not going to commit suicide with you." Honestly, it wasn't like Lil hadn't thought of that plan herself. He'd be the strongest thing they could get if they turned him into their pawn using Gigi's abilities. But when Lil had looked into it, she realized that Ichigo was always surrounded by his father (who had experience as a captain in the Thirteen Court Guards), Uryu Ishida (who had defeated Haschwalth), Uryu's father, Ryuken Ishida (who was a pureblood Quincy), *and* Kisuke Urahara (who was particularly strong in battle). Lil wasn't the kind of fool to step a foot into that den of thieves, even if she was impatient.

"So if we keep just crushing Arrancars like this..." The way the Quincies were destroying the Arrancars was a taboo that would cause the balance of the world to collapse. If they overdid things and got too flashy about it, the Soul Reapers would probably notice and send an assassin after them.

Lil had joined Bazz-B and some others to lend the Soul Reapers a hand, so it wasn't impossible for her to negotiate with them. But she didn't think it would result in the Twelfth Company captain releasing Candy and the others. More to the point, as soon as they realized that Gigi was the person who had turned so many Soul Reapers into zombies and made them kill each other, any kind of formal parley would be difficult.

"Well, for now we'll go back to the world of the living once we clean up these guys and make a plan to—"Lil stopped muttering abruptly.

Bambietta was running down the Arrancars with The Explode. And that's when Lil realized there was something wrong.

"She isn't done yet?"

It wasn't like Bambietta was being leisurely about it. She might even have been bombing more recklessly because her ability to reason had been compromised. And yet the number of Arrancar soldiers hadn't dwindled at all. It almost felt like their ranks were *increasing*.

"Are they getting reinforcements? No, that's not it...."

The countless skull-faced soldiers were piling themselves up and creating a wall so that the core force was partitioned off and protected. They were doing it without hesitation, as though they had already accepted their own deaths.

"What's with them? What's going on here?"

Let us rewind to several minutes earlier.

"W-we're in hot water! What's with that pale girl? All she's doing is making everything explode all of a sudden!" Loly, hiding in the shadow of the skull soldiers, screamed and broke into a cold sweat.

Menoly, to whom the question had been directed, had been overtaken by fear and was shivering. "Th-this is so bad, Loly! She might be as strong as that Quilge guy with the glasses..."

Next to Aizen's two panicking bodyguards, a man was analyzing the battle calmly. He was the Exequias leader, Rudobon.

"*Hm*... Those reishi seem to have the ability to turn anything they touch into an explosive. Because the origin of the reishi themselves does not have explosive properties and she can release them rapid fire like that, planning to wait until she runs out of spiritual pressure would seem unwise."

"Wait a sec! How can you talk like everything's fine? Things are only going to get worse!"

Rudobon, on hearing the half-shrieked complaint, sighed and shook his head. "Those who served with Lord Aizen should not expose their shame for an even instant. You should always be composed. You cannot feel despair when faced with death. Even if your life ends here, you should think about what you could do in your final moments to benefit Lord Aizen."

"Don't talk all calm like that, Zommari! All Lord Aizen's gonna get at this rate are the ashes of our nails!"

"I am honored that you would compare me to Zommari. There is no reason to worry. In any case, I do not plan on dying here." Rudobon pulled out his zanpaku-to and held the blade ready, horizontal to the ground.

"Please observe the ability that I polished to wash away my shame after falling behind the Soul Reapers...!"

"Grow, Arbol!" In an instant, Rudobon's zanpaku-to shifted into something like tree ivy and spread, twining around Rudobon's arms and his lower body to transform him into an arbor. He then created skull-masked soldiers one after another from the branches growing from his back, and the fresh soldiers also turned into a wall to protect them from the enemy's explosions.

"What? This is exactly what you were doing before..." Loly's eyes went wide midsentence. The sand to the front of her was rising, and new skull soldiers were starting to come to life from inside the desert. Rudobon's roots must be spreading through the ground like bamboo shoots to produce a mass of new soldiers.

Calaveras, the zanpaku-to Arbol's ability, let Rudobon suck up the reishi in Hueco Mundo through his roots and use them to create an endless supply of loyal soldiers.

Although the nature of his ability hadn't changed, the speed at which he could create soldiers increased astoundingly as new trees grew where the roots spread, expanding his reach. It was a technique he had developed while attempting to create soldiers underground where the cold couldn't reach them, in response to the time Rukia Kuchiki froze and sealed his branches. The extraordinary speed at which he could manufacture his soldiers had become a new weapon that had significantly increased Rudobon's abilities.

The number of newly created skull soldiers eventually exceeded the rate at which the enemy Quincy could destroy them with her explosions. By the time she realized what was happening, a mass of troops unafraid of death had surrounded the clay-red Quincy.

"I...I don't like these guys...they're not scared of dying..."

In Bambietta's half-broken mind, past fears came back to life. "Why? Why is this happening...?"

It was the fear she had felt when the canine-faced captain Komamura, who had sacrificed his own heart to become an undead soldier, approached her.

Bambietta mostly fought because she didn't want to die. In the Vandenreich, the death that awaited the defeated was called "execution." That was exactly why she continued to fight. She saw fighting as a way to forever escape death, so she couldn't understand someone who threw their life away for the sake of a fight.

When she had fought Komamura, she'd been seized by a fear she had never experienced before. The Soul Reaper had said, "I did not throw my life away, I simply staked it on this match."

In that moment, Bambietta had genuinely felt the terror of facing a true god of death. But now, the skull faces swarming her were even more foreign to her. They weren't staking their lives on anything or throwing their lives away. They were simply soldiers acting as though they had no life to begin with. As though their own deaths were merely part of a system, the horde of skulls accepted their unnatural deaths as they came for her.

They were neither Hollows nor beasts. It was as though an enormous swarm of insects had formed a colony to bring Bambietta into their own cycle of death. That *would* strike terror into Bambietta, the living corpse. The horror, which had been fundamentally engraved into her soul and brain, temporarily activated the scarred girl's psyche, but only to give rise to the voice of fear. "No...nooo...no, no, I'm scared, I'm scared..."

The hundreds or thousands of teeming skulls overcame the unending explosions and rose from beyond the flames. The swarm of skulls used the corpses and living bodies of other skulls as footholds in order to form into a gigantic tentacle that attempted to swallow Bambietta as she fluttered through the air.

The face of the girl who had forgotten she was already dead contorted and trembled like that of a child.

"Lil...Candy...Meni...Gigi...! Help...help...everyone...!"

The gigantic wave of skull soldiers tried to engulf her but then abruptly vanished, following a white, sinister undulation.

"!"

Rudobon and the others watching the panoramic view

from a distance were taken by surprise at the progression of events.

"Wh...what was that just now..."

Loly watched with cold sweat dripping down her cheek as the petite Quincy flew toward them from the ruins. The Quincy's mouth began to contort, and a gigantic maw that seemed like it could take a bite from the sky gaped open. Nearly a thousand skull soldiers were swallowed in a single bite. There were no hints of where such a mass could have disappeared to. Nothing remained under the night sky save the forms that appeared to be Quincies.

"Uh...wah...L-Lil...?" The image of Liltotto chewing on something and swallowing lightly was reflected in the quaking zombie's eyes.

"Yuck... Well, they were tasteless to begin with. What's this?" Lil appraised the meal she had just consumed with dissatisfaction.

Gigi popped up behind her and grabbed Bambietta's head in both her hands. "Seriously, what are we going to do with you?! You're really so useless, Bambi! Whaaat was that? You don't want your reward? If you didn't want it, you should have just stayed asleep. That wouldn't have been a problem for me."

"Oh...n-no, it's not like that...sorry...sorry, Gigi..." Bambietta was once again close to tears as Gigi looked on in ecstasy.

Lil watched them with cold eyes and said to Gigi in an indifferent tone, "It's hard to believe you when you tell everybody you're not a sadist."

"Huh? What do you mean?"

Lil shrugged at Gigi, who was looking at her with genuine puzzlement, then once again turned her eyes toward the enemy. "Ah well, there's tons cropping back up. Are they goblins or something?"

"Hey, are you all right? Didn't you say that eating Hollows gives you heartburn?"

"I'm kind of stuck digesting them at this point, aren't I?" Lil had used her Glutton ability to greedily consume her enemies with her grotesquely transformed mouth in order to absorb their reishi, but it absolutely wasn't an easy process. Hollow reishi was poison to Quincies. Absorbing it was normally akin to suicide. Had Lil not been a Schrift-holder, she would have likely been immobilized.

Lil continued to battle the sensation eating away at her gut as she digested her unusual meal, but she kept even a hint of it from showing on her face as she spoke to Gigi and Bambi. "I think I can do that two or three more times, but those guys seriously had no flavor or nutritional value at all. That filthy garbage pile did nothing to satiate my hunger."

She turned to look at the Arrancar, whose lower body had turned into an arbor and who was still creating skull soldiers with his branches. "Guess I should hurry up and eat something tastier. Though he looks pretty unappetizing too."

"Ngh...!" Feeling a threat approaching, Rudobon groaned. The three Quincies were prancing through the air with Hirenkyaku, charging straight for him, including the Quincy who had just eaten his skull soldiers.

Rudobon tried to send the skull soldiers charging at her, but the Quincy who had set off the explosions had already released reishi to keep him in check.

Weaving through the troops that had been stopped by the force of the bombs, the petite Quincy came at him. As soon as Rudobon saw her, he created a flesh wall from the skull soldiers to defend himself.

"That's some pretty unattractive skin you're covering yourself up with." The Quincy's face expressionlessly contorted like slime, oozing straight to the side. Her nibble, meant to consume skin and innards whole, made quick work of the wall of soldiers. However—

"There's nothing in here!"

The wall had been a distraction, and Rudobon and the others who had sheltered inside had already moved somewhere else.

Loly leapt behind the Quincy, shouting her zanpaku-to's incantation, "Poison, Escolopendra!"

A gigantic zanpaku-to in the shape of a centipede wrapped itself around Loly, and she brandished part of it like a blade.

"Huh!"

The Quincy barely dodged it, and the sand it struck instead started to melt like slush.

"Melt!" Loly yelled as she tried to strike the Quincy again, but the centipede-like appendage disappeared midair!

"Wha...?"

"That was pointlessly spicy. But I guess it was all right."

"Y-you! My Resurrección, you...!" It had been *eaten*. Loly paled as she realized that her zanpaku-to, where she had sealed away a vast portion of her power, had been consumed. Although far from fatal, she felt the terror of losing part of herself.

But the truly terrifying part happened next.

"Hmm." The Quincy scattered arrows around herself, piercing the skull swarm and the branches birthing the next wave of soldiers. Both branches and soldiers instantly dissolved, just like the sand had a moment ago.

"My poison?!"

"Looks like I managed to digest it. Guess my stomach acid was just stronger," Lil nonchalantly muttered as she watched the enemy army melt away. The Glutton didn't just eat her opponents. Her secondary power allowed her to instinctively know how to use the characteristic abilities of whatever she had ingested until it was fully digested.

Although she had once eaten a man named PePe, his powers hadn't seemed likely to work on Yhwach, so she likely hadn't used his specialties when she faced the king in battle. Then again, as she'd told Gigi, "Like I would ever use that super disgusting guy's power." So she could have just eaten PePe in order to get revenge and replenish her reishi.

"So...where are you hiding?"

I don't want to rush things like Bambi did, but maybe I'll scatter around the poison I stole and smoke them out? No, I should kill the one who might be able to counter the poison first.

Lil turned her bow on another Arrancar, the pigtailed one she had just stolen the poison abilities from.

"Eep!" Loly had never checked to see if she was impervious to her own poison. She *had* heard that Barragan, the former king of Hueco Mundo, had been killed by his own curse. She immediately went pale and tried to run away.

But part of Loly's body, her Resurrección, had been eaten, and she lost her balance and fell.

"Loly!"

Loly opened her eyes wide and yelled at Menoly, who was running toward her, "You idiot! You need to run—"

Before they could finish speaking, a poison arrow flew from the Quincy's bow. But before it could hit its target, a huge gush of water washed the poison arrow toward the surrounding skull soldiers.

"Huh...?"

"No way..."

When they saw a surge of water flying through the desert air, Loly and Menoly clung to each other as they guessed what had happened. They had been protected by a water barrier.

Rudobon, who had reappeared at some point, bowed his head deeply as he apologized. "Ah, I never would have thought you would make an appearance here. I must extend an apology for troubling you and necessitating your intervention—"

As though to interrupt his apology, the newly arrived Arrancar said, "There's no need for you to apologize. I should be the one apologizing for getting here so late."

Tier Halibel, an Arrancar whose mouth was obscured by a mask full of shark-like teeth and further hidden by a long collar, manipulated the stream of flowing water with her zanpaku-to. She flipped the weapon as she turned her eyes to the Quincy who hovered in midair.

"Isn't your king dead? Why are you stirring up trouble in our territory?"

"Ha! Who cares why they're here? They picked a fight, so we just got to finish it." Another Arrancar had appeared behind her and spoke as a fiendish smile spread across his face.

Loly and Menoly, who had once almost been killed by this new Arrancar, shrieked.

"Guh! Grimmjow!"

"Eep!"

Grimmjow just looked at the two in puzzlement. "Huh? You look familiar..." But he didn't seem particularly interested in them and immediately turned away.

"I came here thinkin' I'd finally felt some flashy spiritual pressure, and what do I find? Were you trying to leave me out of the fun? That's gutsy of you, Rudobon!"

"I asked you to help me suppress the Quincies many times..."

Rudobon seemed confused, and Grimmjow answered without seeming the least bit guilty. "I'm not interested in the weaklings. But these guys seem pretty perky."

Although he wasn't as indiscriminate as he used to be, Grimmjow was still the stereotypical battle-crazed barbarian.

As if in remonstration, an Arrancar behind him said, "You can't just jump them, Grimmjow. You need to figure out your opponent's goals and abilities first."

"Huh? Stay out of this, Nelliel. They won't have goals or whatever once we wipe out every last one of them!"

"And who was it that almost died at the hands of a Quincy in the Soul Society?"

"Why, you little...!" Grimmjow turned to shoot an annoyed look at Nelliel at those provoking words.

In the desert, where stillness spread like oblivion, a flashy explosion was more than enough to attract the attention of the incredibly important Arrancars. Rudobon's thoughts were choked with tears, and he hid his intense emotional reaction in the presence of these formidable Arrancars, who were top of the class even among the elite.

Menoly was simply relieved. "We're saved!"

Loly gritted her teeth in frustration and irritation at her own uselessness and the jealousy she felt toward the powerful Arrancars.

After the miraculous arrival of the three incredibly powerful Arrancars, the battle seemed likely to become all the more intense. But there was something no one had noticed yet. The residents of Hueco Mundo weren't the only ones who had been drawn to the desert turmoil.

"Uh-oh, looks like we have quite the menacing group over there." Gigi spoke from even further back than Lil, who was keeping a cautious distance from the mass of water.

"Isn't that the prisoner who was in the Silbern fortress?"

"Yeah, that's the Arrancar boss Yhwach captured personally. We can't let our guard down around her."

Lil started giving out simple instructions as she estimated the abilities of the newly arrived Arrancars. "Gigi, can you get your blood into that water—"

She was interrupted midsentence by a sudden *zwoosh*, and a chill assaulted her and Gigi's spines.

What is this? What is this creepy spiritual pressure?

Lil turned to look at the three Arrancars, but it didn't seem to be their pressure. In fact, the Arrancars seemed to have felt the same thing and had turned cautious eyes toward the Quincies.

As they searched for the source of the spiritual pressure, the likes of which they'd never experienced before but that still felt somehow familiar, *something* suddenly appeared in the sky.

A small gate, similar to a Garganta, had opened high in the night sky.

The small form that leapt from the gate disseminated the strange spiritual pressure as it dropped to the ground with such terrific force that a dust cloud rose several hundred meters high. The impact formed a crater far larger than the ones created by the Quincies's earlier attacks, and at its center swirled the dense mass of spiritual pressure.

"What...? Is this spiritual pressure...?"

"It's strange. It smells like Soul Reaper *and* Hollows," Grimmjow responded in answer to Nelliel.

It smells a bit like that masked blond guy who got in the way of my fight with Kurosaki. Grimmjow didn't know his name, but the pressure resembled that of Shinji Hirako, a Visored he had once run into. Grimmjow turned cautious eyes toward the spiritual pressure that was even more ominous than the Visored's.

Halibel, who had been silent, spoke up. "It reminds me of Apache and the others' Quimera Parca."

The Quimera Parca. Although they still hadn't arrived, Halibel's three subordinates could each sacrifice one of their limbs to create that fiendish beast.

"You mean Ayon? It does smell like that for sure."

The ominous spiritual pressure was a mixture of countless components, all mingled together. What kind of monster had just appeared in the middle of the desert?

The Arrancars stayed on guard, but eventually the dust settled.

"Ouch, ow ow... Sand is hard when you land on it. I've sure learned something new!" A voice rang out, breaking through the tense air, and a child in black clothing reminiscent of a shihakusho stepped from the crater.

The beautiful, neutral face that seemed to belong to neither a boy nor girl looked around at the gathering of Arrancars and nodded in satisfaction. But when the child looked at the three Quincies, they seemed puzzled.

"Huh? Quincies? I don't have instructions for dealing with Quincies. What should I do?" They stood muttering to themself before turning back to the Arrancars.

"Well, first I need to do what Lord Tokinada asked." The child, who seemed not the slightest bit nervous, stuck out like a sore thumb. Though it must have seemed humorous to an onlooker, not a single one of them laughed or allowed their guard to break. To be calm in a situation like this was in itself abnormal, not to mention that the sinister spiritual pressure they had just sensed was unmistakably coming from the child in front of them.

"Stop right there. Who are you?" Halibel, zanpaku-to at the ready, asked the child.

Rudobon had been busy creating countless new soldiers. Even surrounded by a horde of several thousand skull soldiers, the child smiled innocently and answered. "Right! I'm Hikone! My name is Hikone Ubuginu!"

The child Hikone was not at all perturbed to be facing the hostile Arrancars.

Watching the Arrancars, Lil said, "I've got a bad feeling about this. That kid's eyes aren't smiling at all."

The child had an aura similar to one of Gigi's zombies. Lil, still expressionless, continued. "And I feel the presence of a familiar scumbag. What's going on here?"

Hikone quietly bowed to the confused group and explained their goals, "*Um* so, I have a gift for all the Arrancars from Lord Tokinada."

"Tokinada...?" The Arrancars were even more confused now that a name they didn't recognize in the slightest had been brought up.

"I heard there isn't a king here anymore, not since somebody named Mr. Barragan and someone named Mr. Aizen disappeared." Hikone's bright tone while saying this turned some of the Arrancars' confusion into hostility.

Hikone simply continued, seemingly oblivious to the change in mood. "So Lord Tokinada said he'd let me become king of Hueco Mundo! Isn't that great? I'll work super hard to become a great king!" Hikone bobbed their head in a bow. The skull soldiers' blades danced, aiming at Hikone's back.

"How boundlessly disrespectful. To even dare presume becoming Lord Aizen's substitute is absurd." Though Rudobon's voice was calm, a tempestuous wave of emotion flooded him as he took Hikone's words to be an insult against Aizen.

Hikone didn't even try to evade the skull soldiers' attacks and simply took the blows all over their body. The skull soldiers' broken swords danced through the air with the sound of harsh collisions.

"Is that Hierro?" Nelliel yelled in surprise. Why would a Soul Reaper child have the hardened skin peculiar to Arrancars?

In the face of Nelliel's doubt, Hikone just looked happily at the Arrancars and said, "Lord Tokinada said no one would accept my claim. Never doubt Lord Tokinada. It happened just like he said it would." Then Hikone drew the zanpaku-to that rested at their hip.

At the appearance of that blade, the Arrancars felt the temperature around them drop. It had a presensce undoubtedly different from that of the zanpaku-to carried by normal Soul Reapers or used by Arrancars.

Before the Arrancars could ascertain the nature of the malaise that hit them, Hikone sonorously sang out the instructions given by one Lord Tokinada. "In which case, until you bend your will and accept me as king, I'm supposed to give you a beating!"

Before the child had even finished speaking, Hikone gripped the zanpaku-to and spoke the name of the blade with a smile. "Revolve around the stars, Ikomikidomoe!"

CHAPTER FOUR

NINTH COMPANY BARRACKS

HISAGI WAS SITTING at his official assistant captain's desk, lost in thought as he looked through past issues of the *Seireitei Bulletin*.

Captain Muguruma spoke from behind him. "Hey, why the glum face, Shuhei?"

"Oh, Captain..."

"Is it about the talk earlier? I guess you can't help getting worked up over that."

"Sorry, did it show on my face?" He had meant to suppress his feelings, but it looked like he wasn't doing a great job of it. After taking a deep breath, Hisagi asked, "Did you know, Captain? About Captain Tosen's—sorry, I mean Kaname Tosen's past?"

"I had an inkling."

Even now, Hisagi was in the habit of calling Tosen "Captain Tosen" when he was worked up. He knew it was impolite to his current captain, Muguruma. But he just couldn't hold back when it came to Tosen.

Muguruma might have understood, since he didn't get particularly prickly about it. "I don't concern myself with my subordinates' pasts. I didn't really pry back then. I thought I could trust him well enough to do his work without my knowing. Looking back now, maybe I should have delved deeper."

"And the Tsunayashiro nobles?"

"I don't care about the world of the nobles specifically because of what they are. Kyoraku, Kuchiki, and Yoruichi are fine, but I don't want to get mixed up with the average aristocrat."

Hisagi also knew about the unreasonable, hubristic Soul Reaper nobility. If they had been charmingly prideful like Omaeda, it would have been another story. But he had seen the nobles' terrible actions earlier in the Central 46.

He'd heard that even the Central 46 had changed their views due to the war, but many people in the aristocratic district still obviously looked down on those in the general populace or the Rukongai.

"It would be nice if they were all like Ms. Yoruichi."

"I think that would be dangerous in its own way." Muguruma imagined a group of Yoruichis jumping around the aristocratic district and scowled. He continued, recollecting, "You know, Byakuya got all worked up as a kid when Yoruichi teased him. There was something cute about it, but he ended up maturing into the spitting image of an aristocrat."

"He can't help it. He's head of one of the Four Great Noble Clans after all."

"Yoruichi used to be too though." As he spoke, Muguruma picked up the *Seireitei Bulletin* from his desk. He flipped through it as he continued. "But I'm impressed you took the job. Sure, it was a unique situation, but I think you could have turned it down and spoken to the other companies about it."

"I'm...actually still on the fence about it."

≡

HALF AN HOUR EARLIER, FIRST COMPANY BARRACKS

"Understood. I will take on the special edition."

"Huh? Really? Are you sure?"

Hisagi nodded firmly at Kyoraku's surprise. "Yes, but the *Seireitei Bulletin* is like a castle I inherited from the previous editor-in-chief, so I'm going to look into this myself and determine whether it's worthy of a full special edition."

"You're much more willing than I expected. Ahh, but you should know that the Gilded Seal Aristocratic Assembly will have their eyes on you if you go digging through the past. I think you'll be able to keep the Central 46 in check if you ask little Nayura, though."

"I'm not going to cover the past. I'm going to look into the man's present. I'll report things as I honestly see them. If that's acceptable, leave the special edition to me."

"You don't have a grudge against him or anything, do you?"

Kyoraku asked as though testing him, and Hisagi allowed a short silence to stretch out before he answered. "Of course I have a grudge. But it's personal. And twisting the article because of my personal resentment would be an insult to Captain Tosen."

He had called Tosen a captain again, and although Naname narrowed her eyes, no one called him out for it.

Kyoraku looked at Hisagi seriously for a while, then shrugged his shoulders slightly. "All right. In that case I guess I'll leave you to it. But you can't push it. This is the head of the nobles we're talking about, and they work differently than the Thirteen Court Guard Companies. He might catch you off guard while you're looking into things and get involved himself."

"I'm prepared for that. And if that sort of thing scared me, I'd never cover shady Soul Reapers."

"Really? Even if an alluring gal like Rangiku seduces you?"

"Huh? Is that really what you think of me? You think something like that would get me?" Hisagi nervously looked at Nanao, but she quickly turned away. He turned back to Muguruma.

"Well, of all the assistant captains, I think you'd be the most susceptible to that sort of thing, after Omaeda," Muguruma said honestly.

"After *Omaeda*?!"

"Oh, but Omaeda has money, so he's probably seen it all and gotten used to sensual pleasures. In which case, *you* are the most likely—"

"No no no! Abarai is more... He's way more..." Hisagi thought of all the various things that had happened in the past—specifically when Mayuri Kurotsuchi told him and Renji that *"I can give zanpaku-to a sex change."* Hisagi realized that there hadn't been much difference between their reactions.

"Let's put that aside! You can leave this to me!"

"Right, it's good if you're clearheaded about this. You'll run into problems if you're too nervous, and we all know what an aristocrat can do to you."

"Captain Kyoraku..." Hisagi realized that the Captain General was trying to relieve Hisagi's apprehension that *something* was closing in on him. Hisagi expressed his gratitude to Kyoraku again. "I understand. I swear on the good name of the *Seireitei Bulletin*, I will do this job."

"Right. If you need any help, let me know. But I'm a lot busier with captain general duties than I thought I'd be, so I can't be there for you the whole time."

"Thank you very much! Oh..." Hisagi remembered that there was something he needed to ask the Captain General directly.

"Hm? What's wrong?"

A serious expression came over Hisagi's face as Kyoraku tilted his head, and he went straight into it. "Captain Kyoraku, this touches on a different topic. May I ask you about one more thing?"

"What is it? It's fine as long as it's something I can answer."

"It's about Captain Ukitake and Kugo Ginjo."

A faint shadow pierced Kyoraku's expression, and a brief silence passed before he replied, "You got me there with that timing. Why now?"

"I met Ginjo today."

"Hm! I see... Right, you don't need to worry about him in particular. Ukitake asked me to extend a stay on his execution for as long as I could." Kyoraku silently looked into the air as he recalled his now absent friend's face.

"Captain Ukitake asked you to do that...?"

"Officially we can't exonerate him, so we're being lenient. It's all just wait and see."

A wry smile came over Kyoraku's face as he questioned Hisagi on an important detail. "So, you heard his side?"

"Yes, but I can't trust it without hearing the other side first."

"You're really an upstanding guy. I think that's good, mm-hm."

A smile of what seemed like relief at Hisagi's attitude toward his own work curled on Kyoraku's mouth, then he sighed slightly and continued. "But now that you've brought it up... Could you give me some time?"

"Some time?"

"Ukitake was trying to deal with the situation on his own. I don't have a full picture of it. But in my current position, I think I can clarify a lot of the ambiguous aspects. Which means there's a reasonable possibility that we'll be able to give Kugo Ginjo a pardon of sorts."

Kyoraku swiftly narrowed one of his eyes. "And on the other hand, there's a possibility that it will reveal a criminal among the Soul Reapers."

"All right, I'll wait until you look into it."

Hisagi then received some casual briefings and permission to cover several stories and left the First Company barracks. As he hurried home, he thought again about the instructions for the special edition he had received.

Tokinada Tsunayashiro. Hisagi contemplated the name that had engraved itself into his mind as he tried to suppress his own emotions. His face was so grim as he made his way toward the barracks that it was enough to frighten Hanataro Yamada, who he passed on his way.

≡

THE PRESENT,
NINTH COMPANY BARRACKS

"Whoa, look at the time! Sorry, Captain, I'm heading over to do an interview."

"You're a pretty busy guy. Where are you heading to next?"

"To the Eleventh Company. I'm covering the thing about the Reio's left arm with Madarame and Ayasegawa."

☰

HALF AN HOUR LATER,
ELEVENTH COMPANY LOUNGE

"Well, that's basically what we saw. Did that help?"

"Actually, we were pretty much just watching during the fight. Lotta loose ends. Oh, and I kind of hate to admit it, but Nemu's fight was pretty beautiful."

Hisagi knitted his eyebrows at Yumichika and Madarame, who had just explained the basics of what had happened. "I already heard that Captain Kurotsuchi was being as nuts as usual. I hope that Nemu heals okay."

"She's not really *healing*. Her new body's supposed to be done pretty soon. Akon's saying that she'll be whizzing around doing shunpo in a couple of years."

"I wonder what that'll look like?" Unable to imagine it, Hisagi cocked his head to the side and didn't venture any farther on that topic. "So, you're sure that Captain Kurotsuchi was talking about the Reio's left arm, right?"

"Yeah, but I have no clue what it all meant."

Hisagi had heard rumors about the battle and had specifically gone out of his way to ask these two about the details. He was trying to figure out if there was some sort of connection between the Reio's right arm that had been inside Captain Ukitake and the Reio's left arm that had, for whatever reason, been with the Vandenreich.

An indigenous deity named Lord Mimihagi had been dwelling inside of Jushiro Ukitake. If that deity had really been the Reio's right arm, how had the royal arms come to be severed? The answer might reflect on Ukitake's dignity, so Hisagi wanted to be clear about the difference between truth and rumor. But as this interview was rapidly making evident, there was a lot of confusion surrounding the situation.

"That guy changed his tune and was saying some pretty weird stuff, wasn't he? Like 'always a Quincy' or something."

"Huh...?" Hisagi once again knit his brows at Yumichika's sudden words.

"No, that can't be right. Why would the Reio's left arm have been a Quincy? One of the Quincies must have gotten their hands on the Reio's left arm and absorbed it like Ukitake did or something like that."

"How should I know? It's not like we heard the entire conversation."

"Madarame, what do you think?"

"It's not like I have anything to add about something Yumichika doesn't understand. Ask Captain Kurotsuchi."

Hisagi sighed at that point, although he knew they were right. "I've tried submitting interview requests for other things like what happened to Kira, but he's apparently been busy for the last half year. He's rejected all interviews. Supposedly he's got a load of new research to do."

Hisagi realized he sounded like he was complaining and let his shoulders slump. "Well, it's probably mostly to do with the Seireitei's reconstruction and Nemu, so I guess that's just the way things go."

"Sounds tough. And it's not like you're cut out for desk work."

"It isn't whether I'm cut out for it or not. Madarame, you wouldn't listen if someone told you 'Stop fighting because you're not cut out for it,' would you?"

"No way. If somebody tried pulling that on me, I'd start by slicing them up."

Before he could sigh at Madarame's disturbing answer, Hisagi remembered something. "Hey, don't you have a younger sister? When I looked up who was currently in charge of Karakura Town, I was surprised that the name Madarame came up."

"Yeah, you're talking about Shino, right? I don't really know if she's my sister or my cousin though. Apparently on the very first day she got to Karakura Town, about ten Huge Hollows got the best of her, and Ichigo had to step in. She's still got a long way to go. I'm glad I told her that she really wasn't cut out for Eleventh Company. Can't have her getting mixed up with the rough boys here."

Though he said it bluntly, Madarame seemed worried about his maybe-sister. Before Hisagi had a chance to say anything, Yumichika pointed out exactly what he was thinking. "Well, even a normal Soul Reaper from the Eleventh Company would probably die after facing about a dozen Huge Hollows alone."

"That's right, Madarame. Not everyone is like you and Captain Zaraki," Hisagi interjected ambiguously, eyes looking down.

He was thinking about the time when he was still a student at Shinoreijutsuin Academy. A Huge Hollow had attacked right as he was taking the junior students out to train, and he had lost a friend named Kanisawa.

Hisagi hadn't been able to do anything at the time, and in the end Aizen and Gin Ichimaru had appeared and scattered the Hollows, and that had been the end of that.

I wonder if I'm as strong now as Aizen and Ichimaru were back then? He admonished himself for the thought, since obtaining strength hadn't been his intention. Tosen had given him a path after he had learned fear in that fight, and he reminded himself of that now. He also brought to mind the name Kyoraku had mentioned.

Tokinada Tsunayashiro. The man who was the reason Tosen had strayed from his path. *Is that guy really going to be head of the Four Great Noble Clans?*

"Hey, what's wrong with you, Hisagi?"

"Huh? Right, sorry. Just thinking about something." Madarame's voice brought him back to himself. Hisagi chided himself as he returned to the topic of the Reio's left arm.

"Did anyone else see the fight? I want to gather as much information as I can."

"Yeah, there was *somebody*."

"Who?" Hisagi, who had been convinced that Madarame and Yumichika had been the only witnesses, asked with interest.

Madarame stated the name of the other person lightly. "I'm pretty sure Yamada was collapsed right next to us. Yeah, he's that third seat from the Fourth Company."

≡

HALF AN HOUR LATER,
FOURTH COMPANY BARRACKS

"Well, uh...I really was just collapsed and paralyzed..."

Hisagi started to think he was barking up the wrong tree as he cocked his head to the side. Hanataro was staring at his face and twitching for some reason.

During the battle against the Quincy Pernida, who was supposedly the Reio's left arm, Hanataro had been seized by Mayuri Kurotsuchi's zanpaku-to abilities, and every muscle in his body had been paralyzed.

"Why are you so scared of my face?"

"Huh? Well, uh...you looked pretty scary earlier when I saw you on the road, so I thought that you might be in a bad mood..."

"Oh, sorry. I was just a little irritated earlier." *Did my face really make it that obvious?*

Hisagi contemplated that as he offered a few more words in order to get Hanataro off his trail. "I've got to go to the aristocratic district to research some stories some stories after this. I didn't know how to get started, so I was a little irritated."

"Huh? You're going to the aristocratic district?"

"Yeah, I got authorization to enter. But I wasn't sure which establishment to start with or what to do... Captain Kuchiki and Ms. Yoruichi seem busy too, and all the Central 46 and Aristocratic Assembly procedures seem like a pain."

He hadn't said the latter bit to change the topic—he really felt that way. Although he had gotten permission from Kyoraku to enter the aristocratic district to cover Tokinada, he needed to receive separate permission to cover each aristocratic establishment. Hisagi, who thought that going straight to the Tsunayashiro manor would be premature, had been thinking of starting with the literature in the Dai Reisho Kairo archive that Nayura Amakado oversaw, but—

"Uhh, I actually know someone who knows a lot about the aristocratic district."

"Huh? In the Fourth Company?"

"N-no...not in the company... But he said he had today off, so I think it would be all right..."

"Huh? Who the heck is it?"

Hanataro seemed somewhat apologetic question as he lowered his head and answered Hisagi's question uncertainly. "Y-yes...it's Seinosuke Yamada... My older brother...I think. He just left, so I think he'll be at home or in the Shino-Seyakuin in the aristocratic district right now."

"Really! Actually, the rep in the Shino-Seyakuin *is* named Yamada, isn't he!? I had no idea he was your brother! He made his way into a lot of articles before I became the editor-in-chief, so I remember him. Hey, what's with the 'I think'?"

"...Unlike me, my brother has kaido skill, so...sometimes I wonder if we're really related..."

"What's the use of worrying over that?"

Sighing, Hisagi tried to cheer Hanataro up. "Don't worry about it. Your kaido reputation is top notch, even according to the *Seireitei Bulletin* opinion poll."

"...But... Huh...? M-my brother might have pitied me so much he bribed everyone to vote... S-sorry, I'm so sorry!"

"Why is everyone, including you, Captain Kotetsu, and the entire Fourth Company, so negative about your skills...?"

I wonder if it's because Unohana was a strong-minded Soul Reaper compared to others. Even as he thought that, just seeing Hanataro's kaido showed that it was more than strong enough. Even though Hanataro called himself inept, if hard work alone had gotten him to his current level, there shouldn't have been any hesitation in saying that his gift for kaido was more than sufficient.

Although some of the feedback the *Seireitei Bulletin* had received said, "His negative facial expression isn't reassuring," most of it was about his skills and attitude, and that he was positive when it came to medical treatment.

Even after the war, he had been far from timid. He had gone with Inoue and the others to the front line treatment centers, and all those who had seen him making the rounds had acknowledged that he was a respectable Soul Reaper.

Hisagi, who had been among those people, thought again about Hanataro's suggestion. If the guy was the top of the Seyakuin in the aristocratic district, there was a very high chance that he'd know a lot about the aristocrats and their reputations. In that case, making a connection there definitely wouldn't hurt.

Well, if he's Hanataro's brother, he's got to be friendly. Assuming it would be an easy meeting and feeling positive about it, Hisagi decided to take Hanataro up on his proposal. "Sorry, Hanataro, but it'd be a lifesaver if you could introduce me to your brother."

He had no idea how drastically that decision would change his fate.

≡

AT THE SAME TIME, FIRST COMPANY BARRACKS

While Hisagi had been meeting with Hanataro, another meeting had been unfolding simultaneously in the First Company barracks.

"Been a while, Shunsui. Since you sent me to the Maggot's Nest, right?"

Tokinada Tsunayashiro had entered the First Company barracks with a large entourage and ordered everyone to clear the room so he could have a one-on-one with the Thirteen Court Guard Companies' Captain General.

"Has it been? I heard that you were under house arrest for several hundred years."

"That's a foolish story. The head family was embarrassed that they had to charge me with a crime and were attempting to pretend I never existed. If that was their plan, they should have just given me an official judgment and executed me or exiled me instead. And what were the results of hesitating to banish a criminal from their home? Just look, that very criminal stole everything from them."

If one listened to just his words, they could be taken for self-deprecation. But Tokinada spoke with a full smile on his face, and Kyoraku gathered that the man was genuinely mocking all of the previous members of the Tsunayashiro family.

"So can I take that as a confession that you plotted to get rid of your predecessor?"

"Of course not. Can't you tell I'm just being sarcastic?" Tokinada smiled wryly then narrowed his eyes. "But supposing that were the case, I am already head of the family. Even if something surfaces later, it will be a simple job to hush it up. It won't be just a reduced sentence like the time I killed my friend and wife. I can make it as though the crime itself never occurred."

"Would it really go that well? The current Central 46 are very different than the ones in the past."

"But aristocratic society itself hasn't changed, has it?"

"..."

"Even though they were nearly decimated by the horde of Quincies and did nothing but hide, most of the aristocrats in the Seireitei still haven't found it within themselves to change. What *has* changed is those of you who have experienced the world, such as you and Kuchiki, and a part of the Shihoin family. Having just two of the Four Great Noble Clans fight on the front lines was laughable. If you include the Shiba family as part of the Five Great Noble Clans, I suppose that would make it three."

The Five Great Noble Clans. They were the first five families, supposedly involved in the creation of the Soul Society, and included the Shiba family, which had completely fallen to ruin in recent years.

The Tsunayashiro family was considered to be the head of the five clans. And once you excluded the Soul King and Squad Zero, who all eschewed politics, the Tsunayashiro could be said to be the most influential beings in the Seireitei.

The current head of that Tsunayashiro family twisted his mouth into a vulgar smile. "Of course I haven't changed in all these years. And that includes my grudge against you, Shunsui Kyoraku."

"That grudge is mistakenly directed. I stopped you because you were headed toward committing a crime."

"You completely blindsided me. I was planning to pretend to be the grieving husband whose friend and wife betrayed him with no one the wiser. But I had no idea that a man like you who chases after women's behinds would be so shrewd and competent. Really now, you did quite a job exposing my crime." The twisted smile remained on Tokinada's face as he indifferently spoke of the past.

"I didn't expose anything at all. As soon as I came to the conclusion that you must have killed your friend at the end of an argument and then killed your wife when she rebuked you, all the evidence was in the testimonies."

Having said that, Kyoraku gave the noble something of an apology. "There's something I need to ask your pardon for."

"Are you apologizing to me? I can't imagine that you're going to say sorry and ask my forgiveness for revealing my crimes, are you?"

Kyoraku shook his head lightly and looked at the man from the Four Great Noble Clans with sober eyes.

Had Tokinada's aristocratic escorts still been with him, they would have been in an uproar over the disrespect in the way Kyoraku was looking at him. Kyoraku pinned the noble with his eyes and spoke dispassionately of his own crime. "To be honest, until I knew the truth, I kind of suspected you of inciting the rebellion caused by Rukia's scheduled execution. I thought you might have been working behind the scenes at Central 46 and given her a harsher punishment than she otherwise would have received."

"Oh my. So was I about to be blamed for a crime because of Aizen? But what would have made you suspect me? I had no reason to kill Rukia Kuchiki. Why, I've never even met her."

"The Kuchiki weren't the only ones talking when Byakuya Kuchiki married Hisana, a resident of the Rukongai, or when he tried to adopt Rukia. The Tsunayashiro raised objections too. If someone like you had put in a word after you'd been reinstated, you could have done something secretly through the Tsunayashiro family."

"Like I said, I had no reason to say anything in the first place, did I?"

Tokinada shrugged as Kyoraku said, "You didn't need a reason. You did it just to pass the time, to rile people up. Especially the aristocrats you happen to dislike the most."

"…"

"You'd go that far just to upset people. Isn't that your true nature, Tokinada?"

"Stand down, Shunsui. Are you sure you want to talk about me like that when you're only the Captain General of the Thirteen Court Guard Companies?" Tokinada, contrary to his implication, had a full smile on his face. It was as though he were commending Kyoraku for getting everything exactly right.

Kyoraku didn't smile back. He simply asked flatly, "And so? What business brought you all the way up here? If you have complaints about the Court Guard, I'd rather you send those through the Gilded Seal Aristocratic Assembly or the Central 46."

"Oh, it's a simple matter. I want you to get in touch with some people for me. Yoruichi Shihoin doesn't seem to receive communications through the aristocratic network. Even the Gilded Seal Aristocratic Assembly don't know where she is. Kuchiki is another matter entirely, but you should at least know how to get in touch with that shrew, am I right?"

Tokinada handed Kyoraku a paper with a message for Yoruichi written on it.

Kyoraku remained expressionless as he ran his eyes down the message. "She's already given up her position as head of the family to her brother Yushiro. What are you scheming?"

"Nothing in particular. I just have a very straightforward proposal for the sake of fostering harmony in the Soul Society—no, for the sake of harmony in the world of the living and Hueco Mundo too."

The Captain General grew even more suspicious at Tokinada's words, which Kyoraku knew he could not trust in the slightest. "Is that really the only reason you came?"

"I also came to see your face. We've been whittled down quite a bit these days, our generation from the Reijutsuin Academy. It's stirred up my resentment."

Tokinada's smile didn't reveal whether he was serious or joking. Then he added, as though he had just remembered, "Oh that's right! Ukitake croaked, didn't he?"

"..."

"How glorious for the poor in the Rukongai that he kept the Reio's right arm in his vulgar body."

Tokinada spoke as though he were trying to provoke Kyoraku, but Kyoraku didn't rise to the bait and instead asked, "Kugo Ginjo—do you know that name?"

"Yes. If I recall correctly, he was the first deputy Soul Reaper, wasn't he? I heard that he was that rabid dog who betrayed the Seireitei. But I suppose he set the precedent that got us our hero Ichigo Kurosaki. So Ukitake got the quality he paid for there. But why would you ask me about that man?"

"I was just confirming a little something. And you shouldn't discount Ukitake's preparedness that way."

Tokinada shrugged again and, as though to indicate that he was done talking, turned his back on Kyoraku. "Nothing in this world is precious, especially in the Soul Society where everything is a fraud."

He took a few steps forward, then stopped and turned to look at a corner of the captain's room. "Oh, and I'll let you in on this—Of course I didn't have anything to do with your mother's execution, Nanao Ise."

In the corner of the room, at the back of a space that seemed empty, a presence held its breath.

"It's not as though I'm the shadowy mastermind behind *everything*. If I'd had authority back then, I wouldn't have made it such an easy end. I would have teased her as much as possible, the way Rukia Kuchiki was tormented, and made a big deal out of killing her. And I would have given Kyoraku a front row seat in the Garden of Judgment."

Tokinada smiled fiendishly at the empty space and then added, "I wonder if Kyoraku would have gone so far as to destroy the gallows for your mother the way someone did for Rukia Kuchiki? Would he have tried to save her even if it made the Seireitei his enemy, the way Ichigo Kurosaki did? I think it unlikely. Kyoraku would have failed your mother. He would have abandoned her. And he would have done it to protect *you*, Nanao Ise!"

"Could you wrap up talking to yourself, Lord Tokinada head of Tsunayashiro house?" Though it sounded like one of Kyoraku's usual easygoing jokes, Tokinada sensed a cold spiritual pressure, like submerged ice, from the feigned politeness of Kyoraku's tone.

At that realization, Tokinada narrowed his eyes, then put his hand on the zanpaku-to at his hip as he continued. "Oh, how frightening. I wouldn't want to be pulled into the depths to have my throat cut. I'll take my leave for today."

After confirming that Tokinada and his entourage had indeed left the barracks, Kyoraku stepped toward the corner of the captain's room and lightly batted at the empty space with his hand. The space contorted like fabric, and Nanao's pale face appeared from behind the twisted image of the room's scenery. She was in a cold sweat, and Kyoraku grasped her quivering shoulders and enveloped her in warm spiritual pressure to console her.

"Are you all right, Nanao?"

"Y-yes... I apologize, Captain General."

"I can't believe you set yourself up to eavesdrop without me noticing. You've grown so much! Is this Lisa's influence?" It was possible that he mentioned Lisa Yadomaru, once an assistant captain and now being eyed as a candidate for the eighth company captainship, to reassure Nanao with thoughts of a familiar face.

Nanao Ise knew Kyoraku was being thoughtful of her feelings. She regained her pep and calmed her breathing.

"You must have been scared. On top of that behavior of his, he has an unpleasant spiritual pressure."

"I wasn't able to move when I was immersed in the late Captain General Yamamoto's spiritual pressure, but this was completely different." If Genryusai Yamamoto's wrath had made her feel like a frog being stared down by a snake, then this recent moment had been more like a snake being slithered on by a slug and melted by its slime.

The bottomless eeriness of that spiritual pressure had eaten away at Nanao's mind more than the irritation at having her mother's memory used to insult Kyoraku had.

It wasn't just the pressure's unknowable nature that frightened her. Tokinada's ability to see through her concealment technique when even Kyoraku hadn't been able to made Nanao shiver faintly as she spoke with what little voice she had left. "Captain...I'm against it...I'm against him becoming the head of the Four Great Noble Clans."

Kyoraku considered how long it had been since Nanao had expressed her own opinion on personnel as he quietly tilted his face up.

"I'm right there with you."

Then, as he thought about the request he had been given to contact Yoruichi, he said to himself, "This has really stirred up trouble—a lot of it."

CHAPTER FIVE

SOUL SOCIETY,
ARISTOCRATIC DISTRICT

"NO MATTER HOW MANY TIMES I COME HERE, I never get used to walking around the aristocratic district."

Mansions, high-class restaurants, and exclusive establishments lined the roads leading into the eastern sixth ward, the aristocratic district. Hisagi sighed slightly as he headed toward the central block where the general populace couldn't enter without an invitation or formal permission.

"You've been here before?" Hanataro asked Hisagi mid-sigh.

"Omaeda invited me and Abarai out to eat and stuff. I couldn't afford to eat a the restaurants here on my own with my salary."

"N-not even with an assistant captain's salary...Is it really that ridiculous...?"

"Yeah...well, I use most of my paycheck to get gasoline and guitar stuff from the world of the living so... When it comes to money, I'm a little..." Hisagi answered a bit awkwardly.

He had ordered his motorcycle and guitar from the world of the living, along with the amp and electrical generator and the fuel to run everything. Since he had needed them all to be converted into reishi, he had racked up quite the reishi processing tab at the Urahara Shoten. As a result, even though he was an assistant captain, most of his salary disappeared to pay off his loans at Urahara Shoten. But he didn't intend to give up either of his hobbies, motorcycle or guitar.

"Omaeda's an assistant captain like me, but he's supposedly got his own jewel mine. Seriously, 'when it rains it pours' really applies to money." Hisagi suddenly stopped and turned toward a dazzling structure that stood out from the rest of the buildings.

"Is something the matter, Hisagi?"

"No, but I think that might be the Tsunayashiro estate." He was in front of an extravagant estate with an expansive roof that reached higher than the surrounding structures. With few exceptions, the Soul Society wasn't inclined toward building vertically and looked more like Japan in the Heian era than the high-rises of the current world of the living.

That aesthetic applied to the aristocratic district as well, but the design of this estate made it seem as though it were looking down at the other nobles' mansions. It was as if the estate were asserting that the Tsunayashiro were the rulers of the neighborhood, with utter disregard for the Sixth Company and the Kuchiki family who served as the district's wardens.

"Oh, that's the residence of the head of the Four Great Noble Clans. It's directly opposite the Kuchiki manor, isn't it."

"Hmm." Hisagi thought that eventually he would have to visit the estate to cover it, but he also thought that it was unlikely an outsider like him would be let in.

At least there wasn't the slightest chance the Tsunayashiro would invite him over casually, unlike the Omaeda. The Tokinada estate exuded an atmosphere of rigidity even less welcoming than the Kuchiki. Hisagi stared at the estate as they approached until Hanataro interrupted as though he had just noticed something.

"Oh, I can see it now. That's Shino-Seyakuin. I haven't been here since we celebrated my brother taking office... Isn't it even more extravagant than the First Company barracks...?"

While Hisagi did get that that impression, it also gave off another vibe. "It's kind of like... The atmosphere is similar, even though it looks completely different on the outside."

"Huh…? W-what are you talking about?" Hanataro broke into a cold sweat, as though Hisagi's serious expression had intimidated him.

Hisagi replied with little confidence, as though he himself wasn't convinced. "It's like the Twelfth Company's Department of Research and Development."

≡

TWELFTH COMPANY, DEPARTMENT OF RESEARCH AND DEVELOPMENT

"Nominate the most important establishment in the Seireitei." Many of the aristocrats and members of the general population would offer up places relevant to the Central 46 or government institutions in answer to this prompt, but most active Soul Reapers would give the following three options:

1. The First Company barracks. The headquarters of the Thirteen Court Guard Companies and the fortification that guarded the central, deepest underground prison, Mugen.

2. The Fourth Company relief station where most of the injured were brought for treatment. Although the Fourth Company had been made light of in the past because they were medical specialists, after they saved so many Soul Reaper lives

during the battle with the Quincies, few still saw them as unimportant.

3. The Department of Research and Development operated by Twelfth Company.

Ninety percent of the high-caliber reishi technology in the present-day Seireitei had been created by the Department of Research and Development. Its founding director, Kisuke Urahara, and second director, Mayuri Kurotsuchi, were indivisible from the Soul Society's history.

But naturally, the director wasn't the only figure that worked in the department. Many of the researchers, at the director's occasional instructions, Soul Reaper requests, or even occassionally for their own amusement, used their acumen to maintain the cutting edge that was continually developing their civilization. They were the aspirational stronghold that swiftly solved all of the Soul Society's varied and impossible demands. They were the Department of Research and Development!

And today, another new unreasonable demand stood in their way.

"Hngh! I'm hungry. I'm hungry, hungry, hungry! Nikooo, I want a snack! Share yours with me! I want a castella cake! One with tons of sugar on top!" The self-proclaimed Ninth Company super assistant captain Mashiro Kuna was flailing her limbs like a child on the floor of the Department of Research and Development.

Niko Kuna, one of the bespectacled female engineers, spoke to Mashiro exactly as though she were admonishing a child. "You already had a snack yesterday, sis."

"Nu-uh, nu-uh, nu-uh! I get to have a snack every day! And I get New Year's money every year!"

"No! If you get New Year's money this year, you don't get any next year!"

A man sporting a horn on his forehead seemed exasperated as Niko scolded Mashiro, who was not only still flailing her arms but had also started to roll around on the floor in a tantrum. The one so annoyed was the Department of Research and Development's assistant director, Akon. He muttered to himself, "Well...you could give out New Year's money every year."

"Actually, why would the younger sister give her older sister New Year's money after all, especially at their age?" Hiyosu, a man next to Akon who seemed to be the fusion of a large catfish and a temple bell, sighed as though he were fed up after muttering his question.

Hiyosu continued, "Just when I thought little Miss Kusajishi wouldn't be coming anymore, you seem to have traded places with her."

Rin Tsubokura, a member of the department, continued to type away on the observation equipment as he listened in. He groaned and sighed loudly. "Is this place cursed?"

Rin stretched his hand into seemingly empty space and, from a small hole that opened for him, stealthily pulled out a pastry.

"Have you finally started hiding snacks in the pseudo-subspace?"

"When all's said and done, she is a member of this department." Akon's reply to Hiyosu seemed to hold deep emotion.

But when he looked at Mashiro, still causing a ruckus on the floor, seemed to recall something. "The actual Ninth Company assistant captain sent an interview request to the captain again. He got rejected pretty quick."

"Why don't you talk to him, as the assistant captain?"

"It's not like I'd be able to answer his questions."

"Huh? We've got some kind of weird activity here!" Rin pointed at the abnormality on the monitor as though to interrupt Akon.

Akon leaned in and observed the activity for a while. His eyebrows knit slightly as he told Rin, "Yeah, you can ignore that one."

"We can? But it looks like strange reishi, and it's heading straight for the aristocratic district without using a gate..."

"It's fine. That reishi pattern has been cleared. The Four Great Noble Clans sent us a direct noninterference notification. So the alarm won't sound either. Of course, the captain is probably monitoring it himself, since he never really complies with noninterference notifications."

Although he had answered indifferently, Akon looked at the numbers from the reishi patterns and furrowed his brow. "The spiritual pressure looks like it's gone down a lot compared to what we observed in the aristocratic district a few hours ago... I wonder what happened?"

≡

SHINO-SEYAKUIN WAITING ROOM

"This is amazing! The furniture and everything look exactly like an aristocrat's estate. Is this really a waiting room for sick people?" Hisagi and Hanataro were sitting in the Seyakuin's waiting room.

Seinosuke Yamada was presently out but was expected to return shortly, so they were waiting. The clinic was taking a day off from general examinations, and they were accepting anything except emergencies. And when Hanataro had said his name at the front desk, they had been led politely to the waiting room.

There was a proper visitor's room, but Hisagi felt nervous about sitting in a room meant for the great noble clans, so he had asked to stay in the waiting room.

"I-I think that this is the bare minimum they could get away with. My brother never really liked wasteful decoration, so I think that the aristocrats must have requested it."

"So they won't even wait for examinations unless the room's extravagant. Must be hard, dealing with the nobility's vanity."

"But Captain Kuchiki doesn't decorate much."

"People say that, but he wears that scarf around his neck, doesn't he? Apparently you could build about ten mansions with what that thing's worth."

Hanataro made a surprised sound, though his eyes remained half shuttered. "T-ten of them!?"

"I didn't know at first either. But when I was doing a feature on old, well-known shops, I happened to hear about it... Did you know one of those hair ornaments could buy *several* motorcycles...hm?" Hisagi had been on a roll lamenting the financial disparity between him and the nobles, but he abruptly raised his head and turned his eyes to the Seyakuin courtyard outside the waiting room.

"Huh? What's wrong, Hisagi?" Hanataro tilted his head questioningly.

Hisagi narrowed his eyes and answered, "I just felt some strange spiritual pressure..."

The courtyard he had been glaring at while he spoke suddenly opened up like the maw of a beast. "Wha...?!"

It wasn't one of the gates the Soul Reapers used. A crevice like a Hollow's garganta opened, and a shape appeared from within it.

A Hollow attack!? But we're inside the shakonmaku soul shield membrane!? Hisagi stood up in shock, but he realized he didn't currently have his zanpaku-to at his hip.

Now that the wartime exceptions were no longer in effect, there were several places where wearing a sword was prohibited even to an assistant captain, and inside of Seyakuin was one of them.

Hisagi was planning to run to the front desk and retrieve his zanpaku-to, but he stopped in his tracks when he recognized the identity of the shape that stepped from the schism.

It was a child in clothing similar to a shihakusho, wounds splashed all over their body.

"Th-this is terrible! We need to help quickly...!" Hanataro ran into the courtyard, still wearing his indoor sandals. The arrival was young and androgynous with a gashed shoulder, several holes bored into their abdomen, and one arm twisted in entirely the wrong direction.

The child wasn't so much on the verge of death as on the verge of being mistaken for an actual corpse had they not been standing and walking. On seeing their state, Hanataro immediately held his hands over the child's wounds and used recovery kido—kaido.

"...Ugh."

The child dropped to their knees and their face contorted in pain.

"It'll be fine. Your wounds will close up soon! Can you hear me?" Hanataro, normally fainthearted, was like an entirely different person as he resolutely tried to encourage the child, his voice echoing through the courtyard.

The child shook their head sadly as tears welled up in their eyes. "You can't help me. I can't live anymore..."

"That's not—"

"I-I wasn't able to fulfill Lord Tokinada's commands... Th-there's no value to my life anymore. Please let me die...!"

"You're just confused. It'll be okay! Please hold yourself together!" Hanataro cried desperately as he continued to use kaido. Behind him, Hisagi had frozen.

What...did they just say...? Did they just say "Lord Tokinada"?

While Hisagi was caught up in bewilderment at hearing the name the child had uttered, Hanataro was flustered for a different reason. *This spiritual pressure is continuously changing! I can't close these wounds with just my kaido!*

Judging that the situation would become dire if nothing more was done, Hanataro yelled, "Hisagi! Please call the Seyakuin staff immediately! We need to carry the child to an emergency treatment room!"

"O-okay!" Hanataro's voice brought Hisagi back to reality, but as he turned he realized a man was already standing right there.

"...?! Do you work here?! This child is wounded—"

Before Hisagi could finish speaking, the man walked over to the calm, bloody child and placed hands on the wounds alongside Hanataro's.

"You've become better at kaido. But this patient appears to be unique. Someone at your level still can't heal this one."

"Huh?"

Hanataro looked at the person who had appeared next to him and opened his eyes wide as he exclaimed. "S-Seinosuke!"

"What?!"

Hisagi opened his eyes wide from surprise too. The man with the sharp eyes and imperturbable demeanor didn't match Hisagi's image of Hanataro at all. The man—Seinosuke—didn't pay their surprise any mind as he skillfully transformed the nature of his kaido spiritual pressure and continued with the treatment.

The bleeding stopped and the wounds began to close before their eyes. Hisagi held his breath as he watched. No stranger to being treated, Hisagi realized that this man's kaido level was far beyond that of a normal Fourth Company member. *He's not even like Hanataro... Maybe he's better than Unohana?*

Although he wasn't anywhere near the level of Orihime's rejection of phenomenon, Hisagi was astounded by the rare kaido skills of Shino-Seyakuin's top practitioner.

Only the child being treated seemed displeased about receiving kaido. "Oh, Mr. Yamada. I'm done for. Please don't heal me...!"

"Not a chance. Forcing life on patients who want to die is my hobby. I won't let you die so easily, so just get used to it. Prepare yourself for the embarrassment of having lived."

"I can't show my face to Lord Tokinada! Just let me rot here like this!"

"No. You're one of Tokinada Tsunayashiro's possessions, aren't you? I don't suppose that Tokinada Tsunayashiro will forgive you if you go about dying on your own."

"Uh!"

Seinosuke chuckled at his words. The child on the other hand groaned and grew wide-eyed.

Hisagi and Hanataro were taken aback by the exchange, but the child, now healed, stood up and slowly started walking. "Thank you very much, Mr. Yamada. I was just about to do something unbelievably disloyal to Lord Tokinada."

The child's despondency made Hisagi realize that they had been in torment earlier not because of the pain from their wounds but because they had been anguished at not being able to show devotion to Tokinada. *Did they even feel the pain in the first place?*

While Hisagi's off feelings about the situation were causing him to hesitate over what to say, Seinosuke Yamada spoke up. "I've patched you up for the time being, but you require full medical treatment. I apologize, since you came to me, but may I have one more day, Assistant Captain Shuhei Hisagi?"

"Uh...y-yeah..."

Seinosuke must have received Hisagi's message from the front desk. Hisagi knew that the interview wouldn't be happening yet as soon as Seinosuke referred to him by name, but there was something he couldn't help being bugged by. He asked in a firm tone, "Hey, how'd the kid get hurt so bad? What kind of relationship have they he got with Tokinada Tsunayashiro!?"

The child, who had started to walk as though the injuries had never existed, replied instead of Seinosuke. "Are you asking about me? I'm Lord Tokinada's servant!"

"His *servant*? But you..."

Hisagi looked at Seinosuke hesitantly. The man had a nasty smile on his face as he said, "Sorry, but as a doctor, I can't divulge a patient's personal affairs."

"Wait a second, there's a ton of things I want to ask officially as the assistant captain of the Ninth Company, so..."

There were multiple things he couldn't ignore as a Soul Reaper of the Thirteen Court Guard Companies, such as a gravely injured child coming out of something that resembled a garganta.

Furthermore, it didn't look like this was a situation where a Soul Reaper had matured into a body that still had the appearance of a child's, as with Hitsugaya. This person looked as though they were *actually* a kid.

If Hisagi had been the type of guy who could turn a blind eye to a child being hurt, regardless of whether or not that child was involved with the Four Great Nobel Clans, eh wouldn't have been qualified to be an assistant captain.

He reached toward Seinosuke's shoulder to stop the man and—

Hisagi's world turned upside down. By the time that registered, he was looking up at the Soul Society's sky.

"Huh?!"

Somehow, the child had grabbed his hand and gently thrown him down. Hisagi's eyes went wide with comprehension.

The child's voice reverberated above him. "Oh, s-sorry! I thought Mr. Yamada was in danger..."

"..."

"But if this showed you that I, Hikone Ubuginu, have the power to fight for Lord Tokinada, then I'm happy! Yes!" The child prattled on without indicating if they were even reading the room.

Hisagi's thoughts were seized by deep confusion. *Hey, wait a sec... What did that kid just do to me?*

He was proud of how experienced he was with surprise attacks, even among Soul Reapers. But the flow of reishi he felt from the Soul Reaper who had just called themself Hikone was different from all the Hollows, Soul Reapers, or even Quincies he had ever fought.

This kid is different from anything I've ever come up against. This feeling... It kind of reminds me of that zanpaku-to when my spiritual power was being manipulated by Ayasegawa...

Hisagi fully surrendered to the feeling of his spiritual power, his physical strength, his emotional force, and all other forms of potency in his body being dispersed, though the child had only thrown him once and the attack hadn't hurt in the least. Hisagi looked at the sky in a daze.

Seinosuke Yamada simply shook his head and smiled as he watched him. "This is the domain of the aristocracy. Without the wartime exception in place, the logic of the Thirteen Court Guard Companies doesn't apply. You should assume common practices that are normally praised as good sense won't be allowed here."

Seinosuke then turned back to Hanataro. "I'll say it again, Hanataro. You should take a break from the companies for a while."

With a smile of self-derision on his face, Seinosuke shrugged and continued. "If you don't want to become more involved in these things than you already are, that is."

Seinosuke and the child turned as if to leave. Hisagi

got up and asked, "Hey! I don't understand what's going on here at all, but is Tokinada really so valuable that you'd let him use you until you get hurt like that?"

The child turned back to him and responded, sporting a smile that gave no indication whatsoever that they had just been on the verge of death. "Yes! Lord Tokinada is a wonderful person! A life like mine can't even compare in value to his!"

The child continued to speak as Hisagi hesitated over his response. "And Lord Tokinada said that he'd even make someone like me *into the king*! I have to spend the rest of my life repaying him for that with my gratitude!"

"Into the king...?"

Seinosuke smiled wryly at Hisagi's and Hanataro's dubious faces and asked the child, "Now did Tokinada Tsunayashiro say you could tell others about that?"

The child tilted their head like a small pet, face paling rapidly. "...?! Oh, ohhh! I didn't say anything! Please forget about that! Thank you for your kindness...*uhh*...sorry, your name was...?"

"R-right. I'm Shuhei Hisagi. He's Yamada—Hanataro Yamada."

"I see! Thank you for your kindness, Mr. Hisagi and Mr. Hanataro! Please somehow forget about me! But I won't forget your kindness! When I become king someday, I'll make sure to repay you!"

Still with that wry smile, Seinosuke led the child back toward the treatment room. Even though the child's blood staining the courtyard was evidence that the events that just transpired were real, Hisagi doubted his senses and wasn't sure if it had all been a dream.

"I don't get what's going on... What's happening...?" Hanataro, on the other hand, was in a daze as he talked to himself. "My brother's first aid is amazing, but... I can't believe anyone with wounds like that could walk immediately..."

Hisagi was lost in thought about something next to him as Hanataro recalled the faces of those he had healed in the past and inadvertently said their names. "That was almost like Captain Zaraki or Ichigo..."

≡

Seinosuke had Hikone lie down on the bed in the emergency treatment room. Hikone's nerves were a wreck, to the point that the child's earlier smile seemed to have been nothing more than an illusion.

Seinosuke aimlessly prayed and muttered as Hikone lay there, unconscious. "Good grief, looks like Hikone was terribly hurt by the Hollows, but I suppose this was within the calculations... Well, regardless, I won't let Hikone die."

In order to hide his true feelings, Seinosuke broke into a smile as he used his extraordinary kaido.

"Even if this child's life has not a single hope."

≡

HUECO MUNDO

"Looks like they got beat in the most ostentatious way," said Shian Sun-sun as she looked at the spectacle in the desert. She was one of the Tres Bestias and had come to the scene late, following Halibel.

Several thousand skull soldiers were mercilessly collapsed on their sides around them, and Rudobon, their creator, had been so horrendously slashed that he was on the verge of death.

"I've reattached all your blood vessels and nerves. Now please rest until you recover your spirit pressure." Roka Paramia, the recovery master Arrancar who, like the Tres Bestias, had also arrived late, healed Rudobon as he groaned quietly.

"I understand... However, I am full of regret. I cannot believe I have only troubled Lord Halibel and the others and exposed myself in such a shameful manner."

Emile Apache, another of the Tres Bestias, looked around at Rudobon, then Loly and Menoly who were receiving medical treatment for their identical wounds, and finally at the large beastlike Hollows that had been pulled into the fight and were now collapsed on the ground. She said, "Hah, you're so pitiful, Rudobon. You let yourself get done in by the surviving Quincies *and* got yourself beat up by a weird Soul Reaper brat who came traipsing by?"

"Hmph...I cannot deny that even if I wish to."

Francesca Mila Rose, who was of course another of the Tres Bestias, heard Rudobon's frustration and said, "Well, in the end Lord Halibel drove them off, didn't she? Seriously, do the Soul Reapers think so little of Hueco Mundo that they consider it a tourist spot or something?"

Halibel shook her head, a somewhat weary look in her eyes. "I didn't do it alone. If Grimmjow and Nelliel and even those Quincies hadn't been here to help, there was a chance we could have all been decimated. We might have been lucky that the Soul Reaper ran away."

"Huh?! What're you saying, Lord Halibel? Even if that *was* a Soul Reaper, there was only one of them! Are you saying that kid was a monster like that flame-wielding old man?!"

Halibel shook her head at Apache's shocked questioning. "The Soul Reaper's physical strength and spiritual pressure were definitely on the same level as a Soul Reaper captain. In physical ability alone, that Soul Reaper might compare to the ice guy I fought."

"So they went out of their way to send a captain here?"

Halibel disagreed with Sun-sun's suggestion. "No, that Soul Reaper didn't have enough experience to be a captain.

That's exactly why we were able to find an opening. But I can't help but be concerned about that zanpaku-to."

"What kind of zanpaku-to was it?"

Halibel thought about it for a while. Before talking about the zanpaku-to's shape or nature, she offered this piece of truth. "The Soul Reaper didn't open the garganta. The zanpaku-to did."

A slight distance from where Halibel was speaking to her subordinates, Nelliel posed a question to Grimmjow, who was looking at the empty space where the Soul Reaper had disappeared. "Are you sure you're okay not getting healed by Roka?"

"Huh? This thing's just a flesh wound."

Grimmjow, whose arm had been severely gashed, clucked his tongue as he thought back on the battle. "I've gotten soft. I lost out on finishing off that Reaper with my resurrección."

"Yes, who could have known that zanpaku-to would move on its own when it sensed the child was in danger. I clearly saw it open a garganta and drop the kid into it."

"I don't get it. What kind of Soul Reaper zanpaku-to moves on its own and uses a garganta?"

Nelliel didn't seem to have an answer and just said what was on her mind. "The next time that kid comes here, I'm not so sure things will go the same way."

"Yeah, the kid'll get stronger with every battle. I don't mind that, but it was a mistake not to kill them for you guys."

After snorting with laughter, Grimmjow's smile disappeared into a serious expression as he recalled his favorite rival. He gnashed his back teeth together. "I don't want to say this, but that was the same kind of thing Kurosaki is. Just when you think they're about to die, they're reborn even stronger."

"Well, other than that, they don't seem very similar."

≡

SOMEWHERE IN THE WORLD OF THE LIVING

In a small country, in the decayed stone remnants of some sort of shine, two Quincies and a corpse were laying low.

"If we were just going to end up doing a runner, wouldn't it have been easier to run from the start? Hey, Lil, why'd you get involved in the confusion and go out of your way to attack that Soul Reaper?"

Lil answered Gigi's mocking with her usual poker face. "I wanted to check something. You noticed it too, didn't you?"

"Yeah, I tried to spurt some blood at that kid, but the zombification didn't work. What's up with that? Was that Soul Reaper as strong as a captain?"

"That's not the only thing I noticed." Lil remembered the arrow she shot while the Soul Reaper's guard was down being cast aside.

"That Reaper didn't just have an Arrancar's hierro. The Reaper was using Quincy Blut Vene too."

"No way?! ...Really?"

Blut Vene was an ability specific to the Quincies that allowed them to rapidly increase their defensive abilities by circulating reishi through their veins. Along with Blut Arterie, which increased their attack abilities, it was a foundational technique of the Vandenreich soldiers.

"How could a Soul Reaper use Blut Vene? That's so unfair! Is it because of that sun pervert?"

"Possibly. He might have fiddled with their bodies. But the real issue is what that Reaper was after."

"That kid was talking about becoming the Hollows' king or something. Maybe someone's hatching a rebellion like that Aizen guy?" Gigi said whatever came to mind as she patted Bambietta's head, who closed her eyes as though she were tired.

Lil nodded at that response and, as usual for her, spouted something disturbing with a composed expression. "Maybe our wishes have been answered and the Soul Reapers are slaughtering each other."

"Maybe we could rescue Candy and Meni while they're in chaos!"

INTERLUDE

SEVERAL DAYS LATER,
IN THE RUKONGAI

As Kugo Ginjo was ambling around the Rukongai, a strange crowd caught his attention. "*Hm*? What's the deal with that?"

Several men in the crowd were making a commotion and seemed to be desperately appealing to the onlookers.

"Hey, what happened here?" Ginjo asked a Rukongai resident he occasionally saw around, but the resident seemed troubled and didn't know what the fuss was about either.

"You got me. But the new dead arriving in the Rukongai lately have been making a commotion about how god told them this was exactly how things would be, and that a new world will be starting soon."

"Are they religious or something?"

One kind of trouble caused by new residents to the Rukongai stemmed from their confusion between their observed religion and the reality of the world after death. Some newly dead cult members would claim, "I should have gone to heaven! This impoverished place has to be a world created by demons!" and riot, so it was the role of the original inhabitants of the Rukongai to soothe them.

"Well, they're different from the usual ones. They always say that 'this is exactly the world the founder said it would be' and already have a firm grasp on the Rukongai and the Seireitei. But they still end up starting a commotion by spouting gibberish about 'a new king arriving in the world' or some such nonsense."

"Oh? Now that's got my interest."

Maybe a Soul Reaper who had been dispatched to the world of the living let something leak to a spiritually attuned religious person who then spread it as doctrine? After making that conjecture, Ginjo decided to head over to the group in order to kill some time.

As he neared, a man in the group noticed his clothes and yelled, "Ah! H-hey, young man! Based on your clothes, you must have come here recently, right?! So you probably know about our faith too, right?!"

"Sorry, but I'm not interested in being recruited." Though he didn't think he would have ever said anything like that during his time as a deputy Soul Reaper, he decided to listen to what the person had to say.

But in the next moment, a word that shook Ginjo to the core tumbled from the man's mouth. "It's been on TV commercials for the last few months. You've got to know about it! It's Xcution! Exs-cue-shon!"

"What did you say?" Ginjo openly scowled at the sound of the name.

What's going on here?

Xcution was the name of the Fullbringer organization Ginjo had set up in the world of the living. He could easily imagine some other group taking the name for itself. But he didn't think it could be a simple coincidence that an association that knew so much about Soul Reapers had that same name.

I don't think Yukio, Rurika, or Jackie would spread that kind of information. But I guess I can't look into it in the state I'm in right now... As he thought that, Ginjo realized that the state he was in now was one of having lost his purpose.

The dazzling fire that had burned within him when he had been alive suddenly smoldered again in his chest. *Not like I have anything better to do. Guess I could play detective for a while.*

After he thought about it for some time, Ginjo spoke to the devotees of Xcution with a friendly smile. "Sorry. I died before that. But I'm kind of intrigued. Could you tell me a little more about your founder?"

At this point, Kugo Ginjo still hadn't realized that he had already been caught up in the disturbance that was surreptitiously eddying around the Soul Society. And he had no idea that bows were being drawn on the Fullbringers from an unexpected direction.

≡

DEPARTMENT OF RESEARCH AND DEVELOPMENT

"The Fullbringers... Now that we've exhausted our research on Soul Reapers, Quincies, and Arrancars, they are our opportunity for trailblazing new technology. I am convinced of that."

"I think this is a chance to return to the foundations of the Department of Research and Development." Mayuri Kurotsuchi happily told the nervous researchers in front of him about their new research direction.

Mayuri Kurotsuchi was the director of the Department of Research and Development and concurrently the captain of the Twelfth Company.

"Our targets are three Fullbringers we have confirmed are hiding within the Rukongai. Normally one subject would do. However, there are great discrepancies between the abilities of individual Fullbringers. Just as our zanpaku-to are different and just as the portion of the Quincies who used Schrift were different."

"Captain, one of those three Fullbringers is considered to be a criminal and the other two took on Ichigo Kurosaki and Captain Kuchiki. Captain General Kyoraku has released a directive that we are to observe..."

Mayuri shrugged dramatically and shook his head at the staff members' objections. "Do the crimes of our research subjects relate to our analysis? Actually, if they obediently offer their bodies to the Soul Society's Department of Research and Development, I will go to the Central 46 myself and lovingly make an appeal for their pardon."

"Won't this cause a dispute between us, First Company, and the Rukongai?"

"It's not as though we're going to *kill* them. We're just doing a little dissection and analysis and asking for their cooperation with a few incidental experiments—no more than the total number of stars in existence! If they already feel remorse, they should offer their bodies to us. Of course, once the experiments are complete, I could promise to ~~remodel~~ restore their bodies to perfect condition."

Hiyosu watched as Mayuri crossed out his own troubling word and stealthily asked Akon, who was next to him, "What's gotten into the director lately? Isn't he being even more aggressive than usual about research?"

Unlike Hiyosu, who used the word "aggressive" to summarize kidnapping and dissecting people, Akon replied with his usual indifference. "It's because Nemu isn't here. The captain has his own way of burying his grief."

"All I can do is pity the Fullbringers he's dragging into this..."

Akon nodded at Hiyosu's words, one thing was bugging him. He asked Mayuri, "But Captain, I heard that their abilities are equal to a lower-level captain's. I don't think anyone below a captain could capture them. Are you doing it yourself?"

"Now, Akon, scientists should never voice uncouth opinions. It's almost as though you are assuming there will be a fight."

The very man who had offered up a plan that would most definitely end in a fight shook his head as he continued. "Although experiments are a mass of uncertain elements, one makes provisions for everything. I have made my preparations exactly for that reason."

Mayuri pressed a button that he had pulled from somewhere, and one of the Department of Research and Development's walls opened up and a line of countless cylindrical water tanks filled with very clear scarlet liquid rose up.

Each column held a suspended humanoid form. A few staff members scowled when they ascertained the identities of the figures. But most of the department was composed because they knew the same had been done to Arrancar corpses in the past.

With the countless tanks of floating figures arrayed behind him, Mayuri Kurotsuchi put on his usual twisted smile as he said, "This is an excellent opportunity. For our first experiment, let's examine them carefully and determine the usefulness of *Quincies* against *Fullbringers*!"

≡

ARISTOCRATIC DISTRICT, TSUNAYASHIRO HOUSEHOLD

"Oh, sorry. Can you move? I have an important meeting starting soon."

Tokinada, who had been preparing for a certain meeting, picked up on the turbulent atmosphere that flowed through his own chambers. At the sound of Tokinada's voice, they must have decided that a surprise attack was impossible. The sliding door opened without a sound and countless blade-wielding shadows appeared on the grounds.

Tokinada shook his head slightly when he saw the men, who were obviously from the same group as the assassins from the other day. "*Hm*... Eight of you at about the power of a seated Soul Reaper... Although as I say that..."

Tokinada quietly sighed as he read the spiritual pressure of his opponents.

"Oh my, who would have guessed that you would come for me while Hikone was hospitalized? What terrible timing." Tokinada put his hand on the sword at his hip as he spoke.

He had long ago ceased to be a Soul Reaper in the Thirteen Court Guard Companies and so his zanpaku-to had been confiscated. But just as the Ise household had their Hakkyoken, the Tsunayashiro family had a sword that had been passed down through the generations. As the new head of the family, Tokinada had secretly inherited it. Or to be more accurate, he had stolen the zanpaku-to before he had even attained his new position.

"And it seems you have quite underestimated me."

Although the assassins were lightly leaping around him using hakuda in order to keep him from pulling out his sword, Tokinada invoked the zanpaku-to. The name had a ring to it that was very similar to his enemy Shunsui Kyoraku's zanpaku-to.

"Offer, Kuten Kyokoku!"

≡

SEIREITEI, THE MAIN THOROUGHFARE

Not knowing what was currently happening in the Twelfth Company, Shuhei Hisagi finished his preparations for the new interview and headed straight down the Seireitei's main road. Since Seinosuke Yamada wouldn't have another opening for a while, Hisagi decided to temporarily postpone his coverage of the aristocratic district.

After the incident in the Seyakuin, Hisagi had looked into the child Hikone Ubuginu but hadn't found anything. He had even asked Kyoraku about it, but the Captain General knew absolutely nothing about Tokinada's private army, so Hisagi hadn't obtained any useful information.

I didn't feel any hostility or maliciousness when that kid threw me over. They weren't being gentle or soft on me. I think they still don't get the difference between good or evil.

Hisagi recalled the innocent smile on Hikone's face even while the child was severely wounded and once again resolved to find out what kind of person Tokinada really was.

And so Hisagi was heading to the interview he had gotten permission from Kyoraku to conduct. Or rather, he was heading to the interview with the thought that the man he was planning to meet would likely know something about the state of affairs in the Tsunayashiro household or have details on Hikone's strange spiritual pressure.

Hisagi had put his tools into a simple drawstring bag, which he wore slung over his shoulder. Coupled with his usual sleeveless clothes and tattooed face, he looked like some rocker out hitchhiking.

Partway through his walk, he bumped into Shinji Hirako, the Fifth Company captain. "What's up, Shuhei? You headed somewhere?"

"Yes, I'm going to the world of the living to cover something for the *Seireitei Bulletin*."

Hirako looked quizzical at Hisagi and asked, "Huh? Is it back in print already?"

"Well, there're still a few months before it hits the stands. But the first new issue will feature a look back on the great war. I'm heading to Urahara's to interview him. If it goes well, I might even be able to ask Kurosaki about stuff."

"All the way to Kisuke's huh? That's tough. That guy never says anything direct in an interview."

"Huh? But..."

Hisagi considered Hirako's words, and a single bead of cold sweat rolled down his face. "Now that you mention it..."

"Wonder why you didn't realized that earlier? Even a baby in its mother's womb would know that," Hirako said, seeming exasperated.

"Well, if you're headed to Kisuke's, you'll probably see Hiyori. If you do, make sure to tease her for me," Hirako told the man headed to the world of the living.

"I'm the one she'll hit though! Cut me some slack. I have to go to the aristocratic district when I get back and gather info on places that are going to be a pain..."

"The aristocratic district? What? A feature on Omaeda's bougie lifestyle during the chaos of reconstruction isn't going to interest anybody."

"I don't think that would be interesting no matter what the timing, to be honest..."

After a few more bantering exchanges, Hisagi left the conversation behind and headed to the Senkaimon.

Hirako watched Hisagi's back before suddenly turning to look toward the aristocratic district. "The aristocratic district, huh...? Come to think of it, Yoruichi's been saying there are a lot of fishy things going on there."

Although he couldn't see what was happening in the aristocratic district from the main street, he almost felt as though he could see something whirling around in the skies above it. He sighed and scratched his head. "Hopefully this won't lead to any trouble. That's probably not gonna happen though."

≡

SEIREITEI, AN UNDISCLOSED LOCATION

Deep underground lay a certain establishment not recorded on any formal map. It was a sacred space where, in ancient times, the Five Great Noble Clans had discussed the objectives of the Seireitei and other important matters. It was the location second in importance to the Reiokyu.

And while it did not house any objects pivotal to the good of the Seireitei, when the heads of the Five Great Noble Clans gathered there, that room became so elevated in significance that the very existence of the Seireitei was tied to its safety.

At present, excluding the fallen Shiba household, the heads of two of the Four Great Noble Clans' households and a proxy for another were gathered in the meeting room.

Tokinada Tsunayashiro sat on one side of the pentagon-shaped table. Byakuya Kuchiki and Yoruichi, who was acting as the representative of the Shihoin household, each sat as far from him as the table allowed. The fourth house had no representative present.

This absence was due to a law passed by the Central 46 that prevented all five clan heads from gathering in the same location as a precaution against the unthinkable—losing all five heads at once to an enemy attack or disaster. The regulation was said to have been issued after the Quincy attack a thousand years ago.

Even now that the Five Great Noble Clans had dwindled to four, the law still applied, and so only three families could gather in the room at once.

"This is my first time in this chamber. It does not seem to have been used lately, but at least it was thoroughly cleaned." Byakuya let his quiet but dignified voice ring through the room. He sat with beautiful posture, in contrast to Yoruichi, who was sitting at her ease.

"I heard it was used in the previous generation to hold an assumption of office. That's probably the last time it was used. After the banishment of the Shiba household, they had no reason to use it."

"Yes, that is exactly why I had this room refreshed. Continuing the customs of the past is just one of our jobs as the aristocracy," Tokinada said in his aloof way.

Yoruichi sniffed. "And yet this place reeks of blood. Did you snatch a kid and eat them before we got here or something?"

Although he was uninjured, the thick smell of rusty iron lingered around Tokinada. His calm smile remained as he answered without denying that he had been showered by blood. "I found myself surrounded by outlaws. I simply failed to avoid some of the blood."

Introductions had been concluded, but Yoruichi and Byakuya still could not figure out what Tokinada wanted. Their worst suspicions were that he might have called them to this inaccessible place in order to assassinate them. But that was not the sense they were getting from him now.

But this is the man we suspect of killing the people in his own birth house. We can't let our guards down. Yoruichi smiled slightly as she observed the new head of the Tsunayashiro house. He was a haughty man who seemed to embody the most terrible aspects of the previous generations of aristocrats, but Yoruichi sensed something about him that didn't match his aristocratic exterior. There was also something repulsive about him that set the alarms ringing in Yoruichi's whole body, something beyond whether had been born to the aristocracy or the general populace.

"This is my chance to meet the former head of the Shihoin house. I see now that there is a reason you are called the Shihoin princess. You are lovely and blessed with both charm and dignity."

"Blatant flattery annoys me. You probably actually think I'm a lowly shrew, right?"

"If you are so self-aware, perhaps as a former head of house, you should abstain from rash actions?"

Ignoring Byakuya's indifferent interjection, Yoruichi narrowed her eyes at the Tsunayashiro clan head. "So why did you go out of your way to contact me and Byakuya? Since you specified me rather than the current head of house, Yushiro, you didn't just bring us out here to see our faces, did you?"

"Yes, of course. I have concerns about the future of the Soul Society. We've been attacked by Quincies and committed a blunder that allowed them to invade even the Reiokyu."

"Now that's a painful topic of conversation."

"Of course, as mere assistants, I don't believe that the Thirteen Court Guard Companies or you are to blame. If anything, the Reio and Squad Zero are the ones who should be blamed, since they were unable to keep up with the ever-flowing changes in the world, locked away as they were in their own bubble. Don't you agree? Had the Reio conducted himself better, there might have been fewer injuries in the Thirteen Court Guard Companies."

Although there was no one else in the room with them, Tokinada spoke grandiosely as though he were criticizing the Reio himself.

Byakuya flatly rebuked Tokinada, face held completely emotionless. "Please leave it at that. It is not befitting for a head of the Four Great Noble Clans to so frivolously renounce the Reio."

Tokinada chuckled and began to spout words, seemingly intending to provoke Byakuya. "You speak of behavior befitting the aristocracy? Why, of course! I don't think I could ever emulate behavior such as yours, not when you moved up your own sister's execution date after you were fed false information by traitors and danced to their tune."

When Byakuya remained silent, Tokinada continued, "Your wife Hisana was also foolish. Look what believing in a noble and leaving her sister's fate in his hands led to! Or perhaps her view of the world was clouded as a result of being tainted by gluttonous, genteel nobles?"

"Tokinada, you—" Yoruichi, face blank, had been about to say something, but Byakuya's hand stopped her.

"It is true that I attempted to have Rukia executed. I do not mind being disparaged for that."

"Oh?"

"However, Hisana was not at all at fault. All the blame lies with me."

Byakuya remained expressionless, but reading his flow of emotions, Tokinada quietly shrugged. "Please don't look so fearsome. It's not as though I came here to pick a fight."

The man who had very obviously just picked a fight lowered his head after those shameless words. "I apologize for provoking you. I'm relieved to find that you are a man who can separate your emotions from governance."

"Hurry up and get to the point or I might punch you before he does," Yoruichi said in a lighthearted tone.

Tokinada smiled wryly before a serious look came over his face. "I wish to discuss the revival of the Five Great Noble Clans. In other words, I am considering proposing the restoration of the Shiba house."

Byakuya remained expressionless, and Yoruichi raised an eyebrow slightly at Tokinada's words. The Shiba household had once been a cornerstone of the Five Great Noble Clans. But when Isshin Shiba, a branch member of the family and captain of the Tenth Company, had eloped to the world of the living, the Shiba had been stripped of their noble standing as their share of the blame for his actions.

Isshin's branch of the family had been totally crushed. The main Kukaku Shiba line had already been in the Rukongai at that time, but they had lost even their nominal standing within the Five Great Noble Clans, which had been just a formality by that point. They were officially forbidden free entrance into the Seireitei, although Kukaku found a work-around and forced her way into the court by getting Jidanbo, the guard of the White Road Gate to West Seireitei, to let her in.

Byakuya and Yoruichi waited to hear the rest, so Tokinada continued. "Certainly Isshin Shiba's defection could be considered the action of a traitor. But as a result, Isshin's son, Ichigo Kurosaki —who, yes, is only part of a branch family but is still of Shiba descent—defeated the Quincy's king. Aren't those achievements more than enough to rinse the tarnish off their name?"

The proposal was more decent than she had expected, so Yoruichi was instantly suspicious of what Tokinada was really planning.

Byakuya, on the other hand, did not allow his expression to collapse and emotionlessly told them his thoughts. "I agree in regard to Ichigo Kurosaki's achievements. However, Ichigo Kurosaki cannot accept the standing of a noble."

"That's exactly it. That guy wouldn't see position and honor as rewards. If anything, he'd consider them a nuisance. If it was for the sake of the entire Shiba household, he might accept. But Kukaku and Ganju aren't thinking of returning to the nobility right now."

Tokinada silently nodded at Byakuya's and Yoruichi's words and smiled thinly as he replied. "I see. Certainly Ichigo Kurosaki does seem to be that type. In that case, why don't we register his sisters as the heads of house? There's no need for them to do any actual work. It can be in name only."

"I wouldn't have expected you to look all the way into Ichigo's family. But I can't see that happening either. Why are you so interested in reinstating the Shiba household?"

Tokinada answered Yoruichi's vigilant question frankly. "Because I want to honor justice. I don't mind using the Tsunayashiro family clout to force things to go the way I want, but that would cause problems with the Soul Society's population. They might think me a despot. That's exactly why I want it to be known that I swayed the Seireitei through fair means."

"...?"

"I want to get the five families on my side, and if I can obtain the formal consent of the Reio, I want to make the Five Great Noble Clans as a body equal in rank to the king. Then the clans would surpass the Central 46 in power as a decision-making body. In fact, I suspect the reason the Central 46 crushed the Shiba house was to make sure something like this never happened."

Tokinada chuckled as he continued. "Haven't you had your doubts? Why did the Shiba family get such a cold reception from the Five Great Noble Clans? Officially, the Shiba set up in the Rukongai in order to build their secret fortifications. But even before they were stripped of their noble position, the Shiba were treated like they were lower than the poorest of the lower aristocracy. Doesn't it bother you that the Shiba family allowed that?"

"Well, it's easy to see based on the value of their house that the Shiba family is as good as any other nobles, so they probably thought that was enough. But what concerns me is that you're arrogant enough to call certain *aristocrats* poor." While Yoruichi certainly wanted to know where Tokinada was going with this, she still answered in a way that would keep them from delving too deeply into the subject. If they got caught in Tokinada's stride, she knew he would lead them far in the opposite direction of the truth.

Byakuya seemed to think the same as he told Tokinada in an indifferent tone, "I have no intention of intruding upon the internal affairs of another family. I understand the stipulations you've made, but I believe there has never been a precedent for the Reio giving his blessing to anyone."

Tokinada's mouth contorted into a grin at Byakuya's point. "That seems likely. Even if the Reio could convey the general gist of his will to the inhabitants of the Reiokyu, it isn't likely that he'd consent to anything. Well, I suppose it is more appropriate to say he *cannot* convey his blessing."

"I have no idea what you're trying to say. What are you scheming, Tokinada?"

"But that era is over. Eventually there will come a new age when we receive the Reio's blessing and the Seireitei—we Five Great Noble Clans—will each separately reign over the three realms. That's all I'm discussing."

Yoruichi and Byakuya both raised their eyebrows. The three realms. He likely meant the Soul Society, the world of the living, and Hueco Mundo or hell.

At Tokinada's sudden preposterous proposal, Yoruichi said, "Before I hear the particulars of this discussion, I have a question. Didn't you yourself say that the Reio wouldn't give his blessing for this? Then why are you speaking as though your proposal is a sure thing?"

"Ah yes, that's easy. Because the next Soul King will have free will!"

"...?"

"...!"

In contrast to Byakuya's immediate suspicion, Yoruichi's eyes suddenly went wide then narrowed as she stared at Tokinada. "...! I see. So that's why you chose me rather than Yushiro."

Tokinada accepted their stares as he smiled—grinned, smirked!—vulgarly. "You saw it, didn't you, Yoruichi Shihoin? The Reio Ichigo Kurosaki struck down and the state he was in even before he was killed! But I can see that you don't know what *that* was. Yes, you don't know what the Reio was from the start. But Kisuke Urahara should be aware."

≡

THE SOUL SOCIETY, IN FRONT OF THE SENKAIMON

"Urahara, huh? I've talked to him about motorcycles and gasoline before, but this is the first time I've tried conducting a formal interview with him."

Unaware of the discussion that was being held between three of the Four Great Noble Clans, Shuhei Hisagi took a step toward the living world, voicing his determination to encourage himself. "Well, I'll get it done. If I can't do this, I can't call myself the editor-in-chief of the *Seireitei Bulletin*."

Just watch, Captain Tosen. I'll illuminate the path for every-one in the Soul Society in my own way. Just like you did for me. Hisagi steeled his resolve as he walked toward the Senkai-mon, handling a hellbutterfly on his way to Karakura Town.

Because his attention was elsewhere, Shuhei Hisagi didn't notice that he was hurtling deep into the discord. Multiple destinies coiled themselves around him, encir-cling coincidence and inevitability. Still unaware that the Soul Society's roots were linked to the center of that con-flict, Shuhei Hisagi simply continued down his own path.

Kaname Tosen had shined the light for him when all he could do was run in fear. Hisagi believed that the correct path was not the path he walked, but the path he had shown himself.

Shuhei Hisagi was neither a prophet nor all knowing, and naturally he had no way of knowing his future.

He did not have an unfortunate destiny like Ichigo Kurosaki.

He did not have the torrent of power that Kenpachi Zaraki contained.

He did not have the deep sagacity and groundwork of Kisuke Urahara.

He did not have a curselike curiosity etched into his konpaku like Mayuri Kurotsuchi.

He did not understand being continuously burdened with responsibility like Byakuya Kuchiki.

He did not have the resourcefulness to control multiple spiritual pressures like Toshiro Hitsugaya.

He did not have the time to lay the foundation of who he was like Genryusai Yamamoto.

He did not have the temperament to sidestep anything like Shunsui Kyoraku.

He did not have the passion to rewrite the justice of the world like Sajin Komamura.

He did not have the firm outlook to stick to his path like Kensei Muguruma.

Later, a Soul Reaper who knew everything about the conflict said this: Because he was *him*, because he was the Soul Reaper Shuhei Hisagi, he had exactly the qualifications the world wished for.

He was walking the path less taken, following Kaname Tosen. And that is precisely why he had the potential to reach his destination.

And Shuhei Hisagi still did not know it.

He still might not have realized it.

Exactly when did Kaname Tosen, the man who had pointed out the path for Hisagi to follow, stray from his own path?

Or had he *never* strayed from his path?

≡

SEVERAL HUNDRED YEARS AGO,
THE SOUL SOCIETY

There was once a blind young man from the Rukongai who sought a meeting with the Central 46.

Several minutes after the young man had been led away by the aristocrat who had killed his own wife, that same aristocrat called out to the guards with a bright smile. "Hey, you. I've got a job for you. A resident of the Rukongai tried to raise his hand to me. Get him out of here—quickly."

Though they honestly had no idea what was going on, the guards had no reason to disregard the instruction. "Y-yes sir!"

The aristocrat's command gave the guards an eerie feeling, but they obediently followed his orders. Even if something was going on beneath the surface, it had nothing to do with them, and they understood that it was better to knock down the Rukongai resident than it was to go against a noble.

The aristocrat said something more to the blind man, but the guards had no need to hear it. The aristocrat was only part of the lowest of branch families, but the guards knew that no good would come from getting involved in the Five Great Noble Clans' disputes.

The blind Rukongai resident, whose throat had been crushed, tried to yell something as he glared at the aris-

tocrat. For a member of the Rukongai poor, he was unbelievably rebellious. In order to make sure the impoverished
man never stepped foot in the government district again,
the guards decided to give him a thorough beating.

Their sadism sparked by the despair on the young man's
face, smiles just like the one the aristocrat had worn un-
wittingly spilled across the guards' faces. They raised their
staves above the blind young man's head.

This time, there was no one to stop them.

While the sound of the staves' blows rung out, Kaname
Tosen silently listened for the guards. *What? What are the
guards doing?*

Enveloped by deep despair and rage, his hotly boiling
soul faintly and gradually began to simmer in confusion.
Though his eyes could not see, he was able to track what
was happening based on sounds and the currents of the air.

One of the guards smiled sadistically as he continued
to raise his stave, but this time it was not against Tosen, it
was against his partner.

"W-why you, what...bguh." The guard who had been hit
groaned. His words were cut off by a blow to his face.

"Don't you dare talk back! You filthy commoner!"

Tosen's thought that they had grown tired of beating him
was quickly disproved by the man's coarse breathing and
rapidly beating heart as he pummeled the other guard. Ap-

parently this guard didn't know he was beating his partner. He thought he was actually beating *Tosen!*

The guard pulled his unconscious partner off the road.

Tosen listened to the sounds of the guards grow distant, still lost in his confusion. Suddenly, he was shocked to hear the voice of an unfamiliar man come from behind him!

"I switched the water in their canteens for alcohol. I believe their actions will be put down as a fight while drinking on the job. That aristocrat will suspect something, but we just need to make him think he's jumping at shadows."

It was a calm voice.

But unlike the aristocrat Tokinada, this voice did not try to hide its swordlike power. Just listening to it made Tosen feel pressured.

"Who are you... Are...are you a Soul Reaper too...?!"

Although Tosen was bewildered, hate once again lit in his heart. He questioned the man with such hostility, it seemed as though he were about to tear out the stranger's throat.

The man made no attempt to prevaricate. "Yes. That is exactly what I am. I'm just a fragment of the world that, in your despair, you burn with hatred for.

The newly arrived Soul Reaper offered Tosen a proposal. "Let me... Would you surrender your hatred to me for a while?"

Though Tosen was dubious, the sound of the man's voice convinced him that the stranger already had a firm grasp on Tosen's heart. He was apprehensive, as though he were speaking to a primordial ruler. An overwhelming power radiated from the man.

The man kept speaking in a calm tone as he offered Tosen a hand and gave his name of his own volition. It was the name of the man who would show Kaname Tosen his path and the name of the man who would make the world his enemy as he reached for heaven.

"My name is Sosuke Aizen. At present, I am still but a humble Soul Reaper."

CONTINUED IN VOLUME II

A note from the creator

TITE KUBO

Currently a manga creator basking in a life without deadlines.
Having no deadlines is amazing!
Original author of BLEACH.
After serialization ended, my torn shoulder tendons finally recovered
with some rehabilitation.
Be mindful of your shoulders when you create manga, people!

A note from the author

RYOHGO NARITA

A novelist who longs for life without deadlines.
Hopes to write a manuscript in Dankai where time flows differently!
(Ends up dead because of Kotatsu and Koryu.)
The second author to work on a BLEACH novelization.
Plagued day after day by tendonitis of the fingers and elbows.
Also in rehabilitation, hoping for a recovery...!

BLEACH: CAN'T FEAR YOUR OWN WORLD I

ORIGINAL STORY BY
TITE KUBO

WRITTEN BY
RYOHGO NARITA

COVER AND INTERIOR DESIGN BY
JIMMY PRESLER

TRANSLATION BY
JAN MITSUKO CASH

PUBLISHED BY
VIZ MEDIA, LLC
P.O. BOX 77010
SAN FRANCISCO, CA 94107

VIZ.COM

Names: Narita, Ryohgo, 1980- author. | Kubo, Tite, author. | Cash, Jan
  Mitsuko, translator.
Title: Bleach : can't fear your own world / written by Ryohgo Narita [and]
  Tite Kubo ; translated by Jan Mitsuko Cash.
Other titles: Can't fear your own world
Description: San Francisco, CA : VIZ Media, 2020- | "First published in
  Japan in 2017 by SHUEISHA Inc., Tokyo." | Translated from the Japanese.
  | Summary: "The Quincies's Thousand Year Blood War is over, but the
  embers of turmoil still smolder in the Soul Society. Tokinada
  Tsunayashiro, elevated to head of his clan after a slew of
  assassinations take out every other claimant to the title, has a grand
  plan to create a new Soul King. His dark ambitions soon sow the seeds of
  a new total war across the realms, but all is not lost. There is one
  unlikely Soul Reaper who holds the key to defusing the conflict-Shuhei
  Hisagi, Assistant Captain of the Ninth Company and reporter for the
  Seireitei Bulletin!"-- Provided by publisher.
Identifiers: LCCN 2020001553 | ISBN 9781974713264 (paperback) | ISBN
  9781974718498 (ebook)
Subjects: CYAC: Supernatural--Fiction.
Classification: LCC PZ7.1.N37 Bl 2020 | DDC [Fic]--dc23
LC record available at https://lccn.loc.gov/2020001553

Printed in the U.S.A.
First printing, July 2020

MY HERO ACADEMIA

SCHOOL BRIEFS

**ORIGINAL STORY BY
KOHEI HORIKOSHI**

**WRITTEN BY
ANRI YOSHI**

Prose short stories
featuring the everyday
school lives of
My Hero Academia's
fan-favorite characters!

VIZ